WHERE ANGELS TREAD

Anthony Ducklow

Beaver's Pond Press, Inc.
Edina, Minnesota

ISBN 1-931646-82-1

Library of Congress Catalog Number: 2002112087

Cover painting by Elena Caravela
Book design and typesetting: Mori Studio
Cover design: Mori Studio

Printed in the United States of America

First Printing: November 2002

06 05 04 03 02   6 5 4 3 2 1

7104 Ohms Lane, Suite 216
Edina, MN 55439-2140
(952) 829-8818
www.beaverspondpress.com

To order, visit midwestbookhouse.com or call
1-877-430-0044. Quantity discounts available.

to my good wife Linda

CONTENTS

CHAPTER ONE

The Arrival of Moses

Nathaniel O'Brien stood next to the mahogany casket in the funeral parlor, staring at the old man in the coffin. The Reverend Moses McDermit lay peacefully inside. The young man, in his late twenties, had arrived early for the evening wake. So early, in fact, that even Reverend McDermit's family had not yet arrived. Nathaniel's dark eyes moved around the room, taking in the beauty of the floral arrangements that lined the walls, gifts from friends and relatives. Nathaniel's eyes went back to the casket and to Reverend McDermit.

"I half expect you to sit up and order me to get you out of that thing." Nathaniel whispered quietly to himself.

He walked over to a particularly beautiful arrangement of flowers and read the card:

May Jesus comfort you in this
time of sorrow and suffering.
In Christian love,
Mount Calvary Church
Lexington, Minnesota

"Christian love!" Nathaniel remarked sarcastically, a sneer coming to his face. "What a joke. Christians are the biggest bunch of hypocrites on earth. Benedict Arnold could probably give a lot of you a lesson on ethics," he murmured to the bouquets as though they were the people at whom he was directing his comments. He chuckled as he envisioned his remark. "You're all hypocrites!" he proclaimed as he walked back to the casket. He rubbed his hands up and down his tired face and over its three day growth of beard. "You deserved better, Reverend McDermit."

Reverend Moses McKinley McDermit. It was a unique name for a unique man. Even back near the turn of the century, when Moses was born and Biblical names were common, Moses was a rather uncommon name. Years later people would say "His mama must have known something when she named him Moses, because he's always been a born leader." The name McKinley came from President William McKinley, his father's favorite president. In life, what the Reverend Moses McKinley McDermit might have lacked in flowery speech or people-pleasing ways, he more than made up for in determination and with an iron will.

Although he had been six feet tall, the way that he stood and carried himself always had made him appear bigger. He was a man who always seemed to have any situation under control, the type of man who commanded respect when he entered a room. He had a presence about him.

Reverend Moses McDermit had come to the Mount Calvary Church in Lexington, a suburb of Minnesota's Twin Cities, from down south almost fifty years earlier. The congregation was a young one—only five years old—and had experienced almost constant internal difficulties. It had garnered a reputation for having a revolving door for ministers either idealistic enough or naive enough to change the way the church was run. While church attendance had at one point reached a high of fifty-seven, it was below thirty now, and the number continued to decline without a permanent pastor. The Reverend Moses McDermit, young, inexperienced, but determined, had been sent there as a last resort by the local presbyters.

Hauling a trailer behind them that carried all their belongings in the world, Moses, his wife Anita, and their two young daughters arrived by car in Lexington on a hot and humid Saturday evening.

Moses pulled up into the church parking lot and turned off the engine. The car spit and coughed once, twice, rattled, and then was silent. Moses and his wife stared at the small white church in front of them, while the two girls slept in the back seat.

"Well, Pastor, it looks like we made it,"

"Yes, Mrs. McDermit, for better or for worse, it certainly does."

Moses opened his car door for the first time in seven hours and stiffly got out. He threw his arms into the air and stood on tiptoes as he stretched, letting out a long, loud yawn. Anita quickly slid across the seat, getting out on his side. She caught him before he lowered his arms, wrapping her arms around his waist and burrowing into him.

"What do you think you're doing? Is this any way for the pastor's wife to act!" Moses admonished, a smile on his face as he wrapped his arms around her.

"I couldn't help myself. You just looked so handsome when I looked over at you. Sometimes I think you look like that actor, what's his name, Spencer Tracy," she said, running her fingers through his thick brown wavy hair.

"Who?"

"Spencer Tracy, you know, the actor... Oh, never mind." For she knew full well he didn't follow such things.

"Daddy, are we there yet?" a small sleepy voice queried from inside the car.

"Yes, honey, we're here. You and your sister can come out."

The back door of the car opened, and two girls, ages five and six, slowly made their way out on wobbly legs, rubbing their eyes and squinting into a fast-fading sunset.

"Is this our new church, Dad?" the older one asked.

"Yes, girls, we're here," he said, running his fingers through their matted hair. "This is our new home."

After the service the next morning, while the congregation was filing out, three men stood waiting for Moses on the church steps. One was tall and had a distinguished-looking head of gray hair; the other two were rather short and similar in appearance, both heavy and balding. All three were sharply dressed, and it was apparent to anyone who saw them that they were all well off and were the money of the church. Moses was also well aware from his prior discussions with the presbyters who had dispatched him here that these men were the source of many of the church's problems in the past.

"That was quite a sermon, Reverend, quite a sermon!" the tall one declared, smiling and pumping Moses' hand. "Especially considering you only pulled in last night! When did you have time to study? It was a wonderful sermon!"

"Yes indeed, quite a sermon," the short men echoed almost in unison. Both men then took turns grabbing his hand and pumping it vigorously. Moses smiled politely.

"I don't believe that we have formally introduced ourselves to you yet, Reverend," one of the short men said. "We are the Desmond brothers. I am Don and this is my younger brother Ron." He wrapped one of his arms around Ron's shoulders. "People tend to get us confused, but I'm the taller, better looking one!" Don bragged, throwing his round head back and laughing heartily. Ron smiled, rolling his eyes heavenward.

"And I am Andrew Sutain," the tall distinguished-looking man proclaimed, laughing with the others. The three men stood there for a moment all smiling, looking at Reverend McDermit. He smiled back, saying nothing. They continued smiling while the silence grew. Ron, with his hands shoved deep in his pant's pockets, began to nervously play with his car keys. Andrew Sutain had that same frozen smile on his distinguished face. Soon Don began nervously stroking his cheek and double chin. It was obvious they had something on their minds.

"First we wanted to welcome you this morning to our church here, and let you know how truly excited and blessed we feel to have you! You no doubt are aware of the trials and tribulations that have befallen this church." Don paused as if waiting for an affirmation. Receiving none, he went on. "It's as if the devil himself has decided to make this church his special target!" he declared, suddenly looking very grave and serious.

"Who knows why Satan has targeted this place for his wrath and trouble-making? The three of us here have had to stand like Rocks of Gibraltar as the storms thundered and crashed all around us!" he exclaimed, clapping his hands loudly together for dramatic effect. "There are some important issues that need to be addressed, Reverend, things that are vitally important to the congregation and to you. I'm sure you are aware that this church has suffered greatly. Many times we were left without a leader. Those were difficult times, difficult times." His face was grim as he shook his head back and forth slowly, looking down at what he could see of his feet.

"The three of us here have had no choice but to step in and basically run things in the absence of a pastor. In the taking on of such responsibilities, of course, we were privy to situations and dynamics that were at the core of many of this church's problems. Are you following me, Brother McDermit?"

"I do believe I am. Go on," Reverend McDermit answered coolly.

"We want you to know that all the information we have is at your disposal, to help you rectify many of the unfortunate wrongs that have occurred here. We want you to know that we will be available at your beck and call, at any time," Don stated, compassion dripping from his voice.

"At any time," Andrew softly and sincerely added, patting Moses softly on the shoulder.

"Excuse me, Pastor," came a voice suddenly from behind them. "I hope I'm not interrupting, but I vanted to meet you before I left. I'm Jake Johannson, and I'm glad you're here." He shook Reverend McDermit's hand, a shy grin on his face. Jake Johannson was a young Swedish man with a large family. The faded gray suit he wore was an indication that he was not one of the elite in this church. He spoke with a mild Swedish accent, though oddly enough he had been born and raised in the United States and had never even visited Sweden. He had been raised in a small town up north so populated by people from his homeland that he had picked up the accent from his surroundings.

"I am running a little late, you see," Jake continued "I vas just cleaning up da Sunday school rooms and came across some glue that I thought ve could…"

"I'm sorry Brother Johannson," Don Desmond interrupted "but you will have to continue this conversation with Reverend McDermit at a later date. We are discussing some important church matters here."

"Oh… I'm sorry… you see I didn't know…" stammered Jake, as his face became bright red with embarrassment.

"Run along now Jake," Don ordered, patting him on the back. "I'm sure your problem can wait a day or two. There's probably a nice big plate of lutefisk waiting for you at home," he remarked with a chuckle, his brother and Andrew Sutain also enjoying his comment. "Besides, I'm sure your wife could use some help with all those kids of yours. What do you have now twelve or thirteen? I tend to lose count!"

"Ve have eight children," he replied meekly. "I'm sorry for interrupting, Pastor, I vill talk to you later."

Jake turned and walked away. Don Desmond immediately turned his attention back toward Reverend McDermit.

"He's a nice enough fellah, and he means well, but hardly a lick of common sense! You know how thickheaded some of those Swedes can be. I apologize for the interruption, Pastor. Well, as I was saying, the information on the particulars involved in these problems is fully available to you. The first situation I would like to catch you up on concerns a woman in the church who has a habit of…"

"That's enough," Reverend McDermit sternly warned, raising his hand.

Don's face registered surprise and he was momentarily caught off guard. He began again, "Excuse me, Brother, I wasn't finished telling you…"

"Yes you are," Reverend McDermit stated, interrupting again. "I'm not interested in any stories the three of you have to tell about other church members. My advice to you is to go home and spend some time on your knees—for yourselves and for this church." Moses turned and began to walk toward the church.

Don Desmond's face began turning a deep shade of red, while his brother Ron's face began to lose its color. The smugness on Andrew Sutain's face suddenly disappeared.

"Wait a minute, you… you can't just turn and walk away from us!" Don shouted in frustration.

Reverend McDermit slowly turned around. "I also want you to know that I am capable of answering any questions directed toward me, and I won't tolerate bullying or degrading comments directed at any of the souls who attend this church. You owe Jake Johannson an apology, Mr. Desmond," he firmly stated, looking Don straight in the eye, "not only for how you treated him in front of everybody here today, but for what you said about him after he left."

By this time Don Desmond's face had turned a deep shade of purple, and a large vein appeared on the side of his neck and began to throb. Ron and Andrew's faces had turned completely pale. You see, what Reverend Moses McDermit didn't know was that nobody talked to Don Desmond like that. At least not until now. Don Desmond was a man with a temper. A legendary temper.

"Why you…!" Don sputtered. "You come here from out of nowhere, and suddenly in a matter of a few minutes, you are an expert on our church problems, and better yet, you have the nerve to chastise the three of us here! May I bring to your attention, *Reverend*" he said sarcastically, "that the three of us here pay most of your salary. I happen to know that the combined total of the rest of the church does not pay you as much as even one of the three of us in tithes and offerings!" he proudly declared, his right hand holding up three stubby fingers.

"I would advise you as your pastor not to say any more, Mr. Desmond," Moses calmly stated.

"Oh you would, would you? Ha! I bet you would like me to stop, wouldn't you?" Don was working himself up to a full boil now. "Let me make one thing very clear McDermit. We three here run this church, you understand? If it wasn't for us, there would be no church. The hard reality is that money is what makes things go in this world. You can preach pie-in-the-sky-when-you-die-by-and-by all day long, but we are the ones who pay the bills around here! We've gotten rid of five ministers before you. We can easily make you the sixth!" he shouted, pointing a stubby finger at Moses. "Now, what have you got to say about that?" Don roared at the end of his tirade.

Reverend McDermit said nothing; he just stood there and looked at the three of them, stone faced. At this point, Andrew had developed a thick bead of sweat on his pale upper lip. Ron Desmond began frantically trying to loosen his tie from his thick neck, as though it were choking the life out of him. An eternity seemed to go by and still nothing was said. Don was calming down now. He searched his expensive suit for a handkerchief, and finding it, began dabbing at his face.

"Ooooowwweeeee!" Don suddenly yelled, shaking his head back and forth. "Things got a little out of hand there for a minute, didn't they Reverend?" he laughed. "Oh well, sometimes it's good to clear the air. I take no offense from the things that were said here today and I hope none was taken. Christians sometimes need to blow off a little steam, don't you think? Well, maybe it would be better if we continued this discussion another time. I'm sure you're anxious to get home and have Sunday dinner with that lovely wife of yours and your fine children. Maybe next week you will honor us by having Sunday dinner at our house! I know the Missus would love to have you!"

Ron breathed a sigh of relief, and the color began to return to Andrew's face.

"I don't think so," Moses replied. "After hearing what the three of you have been up to here, as of this moment you will no longer be welcome at Mount Calvary. There may come a time when you will be allowed to return if you so desire. But at this time you are a cancer in this church, Mr. Desmond, and you two should know better than to go along with his mischief," he concluded, glancing over at Ron and then at Andrew, who began to look ill again.

Don's eyes became slits and a terrible smile came on his face.

"You're in for a big surprise McDermit!" he threatened, shaking one stubby finger at him. "You have no support here. The people hardly know you. One word from us and they will send you packing. Besides that, the money they would give you in tithes couldn't support a doghouse! I'd advise you to start packing!" With that Don Desmond turned his back on Reverend McDermit and walked away.

Andrew Sutain and Ron Desmond stood there for a moment, both appearing on the verge of tears.

"I don't know what to say..." Andrew began and then stopped. Ron Desmond's eyes met Moses' for a moment, and then looked at the ground.

"Maybe it's time we all went home," Moses said.

The two men nodded, turned, and left. Pastor McDermit, still stone faced, watched them disappear around the corner. He was all alone now. He walked through the doors of his church, knelt at the front pew, put his head in his hands and wept.

Things didn't turn out as Don Desmond had planned. Of course he had immediately contacted everyone in the church to persuade them to take a vote to oust the new pastor. The other five ministers who had pastored there had either left because of Don's intimidating tactics or because they had become overwhelmingly discouraged by their apparent inability to change the situation. Nevertheless, Moses had heard of what Don was up to, and the next Sunday he asked the congregation to vote on whether he should remain as their pastor. The vote was seventeen yeas, zero nays.

Don Desmond took the news hard. For all his bullying, exaggerating, and intimidating behavior, Don had been under the impression that he was a church leader and the one who had been holding the church together. He had, in fact, poured much of his own time and money into remodeling the building in which they were holding services. When he heard that not one member had voted as he had instructed, it was a devastating blow.

As the months went by, Ron Desmond and Andrew Sutain, after meeting with Reverend McDermit, started attending the services again with their families. This hit Don even harder, considering he had admonished his brother to never set foot in that church again. Ron, despite the rift between him and his brother, seemed to be at peace with himself. "I came to realize, after that confrontation in front of the church," Ron later told Moses "that what we were doing, and what we had been doing, was wrong. No one, including me, had ever stood up to my brother like that before. I guess it was something that needed to happen. It's strange, but it was almost like I had spiritual blinders on, and then suddenly they were removed as we were standing in front of the church. It's the oddest thing. Up until that moment, I was one hundred percent certain we had been doing the right thing. I love my brother, but I realized I had to put God first."

A couple years went by, and the church began to blossom under the strong and steady hand of Reverend McDermit. It seemed that there was a new face at almost every service, and attendance was now running between sixty and seventy.

Then, early one morning, Ron Desmond came rushing into Reverend McDermit's office. "My brother… he had a heart attack last night, Reverend McDermit! The doctors are telling us it doesn't look good. Will you come down to the hospital with me?"

The request caught Moses momentarily off guard. "Sure, Ron, I can, but are you sure your brother would want me there?" he asked softly.

"Yes, Reverend, that's why I'm here! He's been asking for you! Can you come right now?"

Reverend McDermit grabbed his hat and within a half-hour they were at the hospital. The doctor greeted them outside of Don's room.

"I take it you are Reverend McDermit?"

"Yes, I am; how is Don?"

"I'd like to tell you he will be fine, but that's not the case. Mr. Desmond has suffered a severe heart attack that would be dangerous for anybody, but for him doubly so because of his excessive weight. Frankly, I'm surprised he's alive. Normally I wouldn't allow visitors, but he has insisted on seeing you from the start. I need him to calm down and rest, and I'm hoping that after he has seen you, he will relax."

"Pastor McDermit, Don told me that he wanted to see you," Ron said. "Alone."

Moses took off his hat, holding it with both hands in front of him, stroking the rim with his thumbs as he walked slowly into the hospital room. The room was dark, and it had the cold antiseptic smell that all hospital rooms seem to have. Don Desmond was lying still in his bed, a sheet pulled up to his chest. His face and arms were white, and he appeared to be asleep. But as soon as Moses came within a foot of his bed, he slowly opened his eyes.

"Hello, Pastor," he whispered weakly, a small smile slowly coming to his face.

"Hello, Don," Moses answered, putting his hand on Don's hand. "How are you feeling?"

"Wonderful," he whispered, a bigger smile trying to work itself across his face. "I needed to talk to you about some of the things I have said and done. I wanted to say that I am sorry. I know I have caused many people a lot of pain and trouble. I needed to tell you what happened to me... about what I saw..." Don closed his eyes and took some deep breaths.

"That's okay, Don, you don't have to say anymore," Moses said, patting his hand.

"No... this is important to me, please don't stop me." He began again. "For some time I knew what I wanted to do and say to you, to make things right. But I just couldn't get myself to do it. Something always seemed to hold me back. I thought that it was just my pride, but I felt powerless, almost like something had a hold on me." Don paused and closed his eyes for a moment.

"Why don't you rest now, Don, we can talk later. You really shouldn't talk right now."

"Don't try to stop me, Reverend, you know how stubborn I am."

"Yes I do. Go ahead, Don," Moses relented, his eyes tearing up. "I won't try to stop you again."

"Yesterday, when I was in my office, I began to feel strange. Suddenly, my shoulder started aching something terrible. Then I felt this tremendous pressure on my chest. I started gasping for breath and began sinking to the floor. My secretary came running over to me, and pretty soon the whole office staff was around me. They laid me on my back, and when I looked up at all the people standing around me, that's when I saw them." His eyes opened wide, and he seemed to be looking right through Moses.

"Saw whom?" Moses questioned.

"They were all around me, whispering, talking, laughing. They were all around the people who work with me." Don's lip began to tremble, and he began to cry. "I'm so ashamed Pastor, I'm so sorry for the trouble I have caused you. I had no idea. Will you forgive me?"

"Of course I do, Don. I forgave you a long time ago," Moses answered through his own tears.

A wave of relief seemed to sweep over Don. "Will you pray with me, Pastor?" he asked quietly.

For the next few minutes, Moses and Don prayed together. The two men then continued their discussion in hushed tones, with Don, despite his condition, doing most of the talking. Moses would nod occasionally to affirm that he understood what Don was telling him. Finally, the doctor stepped into the room and informed them that Mr. Desmond needed his rest and it was time for Moses to go. As Moses turned to leave, Don lifted his hand and motioned to him to come back. He grabbed Moses' hand, squeezed it tightly and whispered:

"Keep it up Pastor. Fight them."

CHAPTER TWO

Deep Calleth Unto Deep

Don Desmond died that evening. The funeral service was held at the church and Moses preached the most wonderful eulogy anyone had ever heard. It was a great time of healing for the church and for Don's family. It was a miracle, really, considering the shape that everything had been in just a few short years earlier.

And so, for the next four decades the church blossomed, guided by the strong and steady hand of Reverend Moses McDermit. What had started out as a small struggling congregation became a healthy, thriving body; one that needed to construct three additions to the building. Attendance reached three hundred, and for the first time during his ministry, Moses began to consider hiring an assistant, because he simply could not meet the needs of all those people by himself. He was also getting on in years. His hair was still thick and wavy, but it was now as white as snow. He had a hard time coming to terms with growing older, but age had begun to slow him down. He mentioned the idea of an assistant pastor to the church board and then sent the word out to some of his fellow ministers around the country. While his search for an assistant was really no secret, he never formally announced it to the congregation. Moses was overprotective in that way, never wanting to alarm or disturb them.

Not long after that, Reverend Charlie Fitch was invited to speak at the church. He was to preach during a mid week service, and again, even though it was never announced, everyone in the congregation knew he was there to try out for the position of assistant pastor. He was a handsome man, a southern preacher, in his early thirties. He stood an impressive six-foot-four and had a smile that could light up a room. He brought with him his beautiful and bubbly wife, Jennifer, who sang like a bird. Together, they were an impressive pair, and charisma poured out of both of them like a fountain. Lightning struck as Reverend Fitch began to preach, and if there is such a thing as love at first sight, then this was love at first sight between a congregation and a preacher. With big toothy smiles the Fitches sang, they laughed, they charmed the congregation.

"Hallelujah, it's good to be here!" he announced loudly. If he said it once, he said it ten times during the course of the evening. And each time he made that proclamation, it was met with a progressively louder "Amen!" that literally shook the walls of the old church.

Before the service was over, Reverend McDermit strode up next to Reverend Fitch at the microphone and put his arm around his shoulder. "I know that it was never announced, but for some time, we at Mount Calvary have been considering hiring an assistant minister here. There is nothing wrong with me. My health is fine, but the Lord has blessed this church so abundantly that one man can no longer possibly meet all the needs of this congregation. Tonight, we have been blessed with the preaching and singing of this wonderful couple here," he declared, patting Reverend Fitch on the back. "I know that this decision is not only mine, but by your response tonight, I think that it's apparent we don't have to look any further," he stated, motioning to Reverend Fitch's wife to come and stand next to them at the pulpit. Reverend McDermit leaned forward into the microphone and declared, "Meet the new assistant pastor!"

A resounding cheer arose from the assembly, followed by loud applause.

"Let's give God the glory!" Reverend Fitch shouted as he pointed heavenward. The applause grew almost deafening.

The church did put it to a vote, but it was only a formality. In fact, of the 296 people that were in attendance that night, there were only two nay votes. Since the voting was done on secret ballot, the identities of the dissenters were unknown and seemingly unimportant.

The Fitches immediately jumped in with both feet. They were a welcome addition to the church, for the age gap between Moses McDermit and his congregation had grown wider over the years. This was a young and growing congregation, and many of the church people enjoyed having a minister closer to their own ages.

There were very few people left who had been with Moses McDermit from the beginning of his pastorate on that warm August day now so long ago. Most had either died or retired to a warm climate. The church began to relate to this young, charismatic couple in a way that Reverend Moses McDermit couldn't.

But even in his prime, Reverend McDermit had never been that type of minister. He had led more by example, by his presence, a strong pillar that could withstand any storm, someone who was always there when trouble came. When the phone rang at three o'clock in the morning and someone's child had a fever of 105, he would be waiting at the hospital before the parents arrived. When he would hear that a family had come on hard times, a $50 bill might be slipped discreetly into a mother's hand or a father's suit jacket after a church service. When someone would come along and suddenly reveal to the congregation some new "revelation" that might have caused a church split if left to grow, he would quietly pull that member aside and straighten him out. If they refused, they were sent politely but firmly on their way. Moses was self-disciplined, and expected much from himself in his role of pastor, and in return expected much from his congregation. He never learned the art of sugarcoating his words, or buttering up to people. He led by example and with wisdom.

Two years went by. Moses' wife, Anita, discovered a lump in her breast and was diagnosed with cancer. It was fast growing, and within a matter of weeks she was hospitalized.

"You are the only man I have ever loved, Moses McDermit," she proclaimed to him from her hospital bed. He lay his head gently on her lap and she ran her fingers once again through his wavy white hair.

"I was so lucky that God blessed me with you. You're the kind of man who comes along once in a lifetime. We have had a wonderful life together, you and me and the children. It does go by so quickly though, doesn't it Moses?"

"Don't talk like that Anita; we still have many years together," he argued, trying to hold back his emotions for fear he would lose control of himself.

"Reverend McDermit," she said in a lecturing tone with a smile on her face, "as long as I've known you, you have never been one to run from the truth or avoid something because it's unpleasant. We both know that I am dying, and I should say I don't like it any more than you do. But haven't we both looked forward to the day when we will be with the Lord?"

"Yes… yes we have. But I love you so much, Anita, I am afraid that this may be too much for me to bear." The tears started to flow freely now, and he buried his face into her.

"You will bear it, Moses. That is one thing I am sure of. And I will wait for you, on the other side, where we will always be together."

Within months, after much pain and suffering, Anita passed away.

After the funeral, Moses was essentially alone. Their two daughters had married and moved away years before. He began to spend even more time at the church than he usually did. While the church and church work had always been Moses' primary focus, it now became his whole life. He was there almost from daybreak to sunset, reading commentaries, counseling, setting up meetings with this group or that group.

The truth was that for the first time in his life, Moses McDermit was lonely. He was the one now who really needed someone, and he thrived on his interactions with the church people and his pastoral duties.

Moses was in his seventies now, and he had earned the right to retire and move south to a warmer climate. Although he was a generous man with his money, he also knew the value of a dollar and had invested money wisely over the years, for himself and his church. Really, there was no reason why he could not leave behind a job well done and bask under a warm southern sun. And although he was still relatively healthy, there were times when he couldn't do the job as well as he used to do, or wanted to do. His problem, the thing that made the very thought of retirement so distasteful, was that deep down, inside and out, he was not just Moses McDermit. He was Reverend Moses McDermit. He loved his God, his church, and his work as much as he cherished life itself. He existed because of that devotion. He felt that the work to which God had called him knew no time limit, no age barrier. He must be, he had to be, Reverend Moses McDermit to his last breath.

It was at this critical time in Moses' life that Nathaniel O'Brien walked through the doors of Mount Calvary Church. Nathaniel was a single man, of medium height, stocky, with a shock of black hair on his head. His dark, rugged good looks favored his mother, who was full-blooded Italian. He had the body of a construction worker, which is how he made his living much of the time, although in Minnesota, with its severe weather, he would also find work as a handyman in the off season. It was during one off his lay-offs that he happened to be driving by the church one bitterly cold January night.

Moses was about midway through his Sunday evening sermon. Nathaniel had hardly been in a church before, but at that point in his life, he was vaguely aware that something was missing in his life, something he was not finding with friends, women, and barrooms. There was no special reason that he had even picked this church. He just happened to be driving by it one evening and went in.

"The Lord will never leave you or forsake you!" Nathaniel heard Moses exhort as he quickly found a seat near the back of the church.

"Let me tell you something right now," Moses went on, "You may have friends, friends who are as near and dear to you as family, friends you feel you could rely on through thick and thin. You may never have a shadow of a doubt that if trouble came, they would stand behind you. It is said that if a person were lucky, he might have one friend in his lifetime who would fit this description; an extremely lucky person might have two. But even so, let me warn you, even those people can fail you, disappoint you. They don't mean to, they just do, they're fallible, and it can break your heart. But there is someone who will never leave you," Moses was preaching now, his voice slowly rising with emotion.

"Someone who will never disappoint you! Someone who will never forsake you! Someone who sticks closer than a brother! Someone who cares for you so much that he knows the very number of hairs on your head!" Nathaniel ran his fingers through his thick head of hair.

"This someone has known you from the foundation of the world, and this friend knows that unless he comes to your aid in your hour of trouble, in your hour of need, you would surely die. This man, this friend," Moses expounded pulling his handkerchief from his coat pocket and wiping his forehead, "this Jesus Christ, forfeited his life for you, taking your place on the cross. He braved all the beatings and wickedness that man could give, and then stood up to all the demons from hell at Calvary to purchase your freedom! Only he is the kind of friend in whom you can put your complete trust!"

These words made Nathaniel feel odd. He thought that maybe he was just tired and he rubbed his face. To his surprise his face was wet, wet with tears. Nathaniel was the type who never cried. In fact, the last time he had wept was probably sometime during childhood. Then what was this? Odd, he thought. How could someone cry without knowing it? But even if Nathaniel's mind could not comprehend what was happening, the ache within him did. Something deep inside called to him, something he had not even realized was there.

"In Psalms, it says that deep calleth unto deep," Moses continued, holding up his Bible. "What that means is that something inside all of us, at the very core of our being, yearns for a relationship with God. I have heard it said that everyone's heart is created with a God-shaped void and that it can be filled only by God. People will try to fill this void with many things: promiscuity, love, drugs, hate, relationships, sports, politics, and even, strangely enough, religion. Some things may even seem to fit for a while, maybe even for a few years, but the feeling always returns, the thirst that can't be quenched. We try to cram every imaginable thing under the sun to fill this ache we carry, this emptiness. But I need to tell you, that there is only one shape that will fit in that secret place. That shape is made in the image of the one who gave his life for you on Calvary, Jesus Christ!"

By now Nathaniel was bent over in his pew, with his head in his hands. He felt a warmth sweeping over him, touching the thing inside him that only a few moments before he had hardly known existed. "Deep calleth unto deep, deep calleth unto deep…" seemed to whisper over and over in Nathaniel's head and heart.

"I understand," he quietly said to himself. "I understand, Lord."

CHAPTER THREE

Greater is He

From that day forward Nathaniel began attending church at Mount Calvary and started walking with God.

"So you say your name is O'Brien, is it?" Moses asked, putting on an Irish accent and looking suspiciously at Nathaniel's dark hair and features.

"Well, you must be from the far southern end of the Old Sod then. We McDermits have never seen the likes of this!" he said patting Nathaniel gently on the head.

Nathaniel took to Reverend McDermit right away. Besides his subtle sense of humor, Moses appealed to Nathaniel because he minced no words, and without being cruel, said things that needed to be said. He also took pleasure in the fact that at times Moses could become a little ornery, sometimes saying or doing things that made people squirm in their seats, or feel a little uncomfortable. But whatever he did, it always seemed to end up to be what was needed at that moment. Pure and simple, even though Moses was getting up there in years, he was still a man's man. He surely would never be labeled a sensitive modern male, and that's exactly what Nathaniel liked about him.

When it came to Reverend Fitch and his wife—they were nice enough people, he thought. The services in which they sang and preached were always full of excitement. Their singing, hand-clapping, and hand-shaking unquestionably got the congregation moving, and they certainly filled a need in the church. But the difference for Nathaniel was that even though the Fitches could leave him feeling as if his next step might be on streets of gold, it was Reverend McDermit who left him thinking, contemplating, and growing.

That first year Nathaniel found himself waiting around after many of the church services, talking to Reverend McDermit, gleaning Biblical knowledge, and absorbing much of the wisdom held within the aging man's mind. Moses was more than happy to take the time to teach such an eager student. Nathaniel's curiosity and excitement brought joy to his heart, and Nathaniel's rough edges were a source of amusement to him, for Nathaniel pulled no punches when asking questions or making judgments.

Soon, another year had passed and Nathaniel began volunteering to do the odd jobs around Moses' house. Nathaniel cut the grass, changed the oil in Moses' car, and raked the leaves. In a way, Nathaniel felt that it earned him the right to take so much of Moses' time with asking questions.

One warm fall day, Nathaniel was over at Moses' house helping replace some rotting wood on the eaves of the garage and painting the new ones. As usual the conversation centered on the great theological and philosophical questions of all time. It began as they were tearing down the rotted boards and continued on as they painted and later as they cleaned the brushes.

"Nathaniel, since I've known you, I think you've asked me every question under the sun, from the old standby 'If God made a rock too heavy to lift, could he lift it?' to 'If God knew man would fail, why did he create him in the first place?' Even though you've got a lot of questions, I see a childlike faith in you, combined with a strong sense of right and wrong that I find very refreshing. I've got to warn you though, and I hesitate to even say it, but the faith you have right now will not be easy to keep. The world has a way of wearing you down, turning you cynical. If you can hold on to that first love you have, that faith, you will have the potential to do great things for the Lord."

Nathaniel felt his chest swelling with pride.

"But," he continued, taking Nathaniel's right hand and holding it up, "something tells me that in the past you may have acted a little too quickly during certain situations and made rash judgements. Maybe taking matters into your own hands?" he asked, running his fingers over Nathaniel's scarred knuckles.

"Do you mean these marks? Most are very old, and besides, how do you know I didn't get these scars on my hand from doing construction work?" Nathaniel entreated with a wry smile.

"Maybe," answered Moses, "but what about this?" pointing to the bend in the bridge of Nathaniel's nose. "And this?" pointing to a light scar near the side of his left eye.

"Well, there is a good story behind every one of those," Nathaniel protested, still smiling.

"There usually is, Nathaniel. That's the problem. People can always come up with an explanation or a reason for their actions, why they needed to tell this person off, bring a lawsuit against that person, or punch someone in the nose," Moses explained, emphasizing "nose" with a rap of his hammer on the paint lid, securing it.

"Human beings have a remarkable capacity to rationalize even their most wretched behavior. What's even worse is when someone who calls himself a Christian searches scripture to justify his actions. He will take a sentence or a paragraph out of context, declare that the 'Lord is on my side' and do horrible things to other people. I've seen it happen many times, Nathaniel. When someone reaches that point he can almost never be reasoned with or changed—his conscience has been seared and only the Lord can change him. I am not saying that there is never a time to stand up and fight for what you believe. I've had to do it more times than I like to recall, but it should be a last resort. Maybe you have conquered this impulse—only you know that. But something tells me you must be careful, my friend, because the enemy knows your weaknesses better than even you do."

For a moment Nathaniel was stunned into silence. The arrow of truth had deflated his swelling chest, and it hurt more than any punch in the nose he had ever received.

"Well, Reverend, you sure don't beat around the bush, do you?" he sputtered, his smile now hiding his embarrassment. "I suppose it wouldn't help my case if I stomped off in anger right now, would it?" Both men laughed.

"First, I will admit," Nathaniel continued, "I have been in my share of fights and barroom brawls. I grew up that way. But in my defense, all of those types of disagreements I had occurred before I started attending church. I'm a new man now, so don't you think that maybe you're comparing apples to oranges? I won't be in the same situations, and I don't have the same attitude. Oh, I know that I still have a few rough edges, but they're smoothing themselves out. But one thing that you said I didn't understand. When you said 'Be careful, because the enemy knows your weaknesses better than you do.' What did you mean by that? I don't have any enemies in church."

Reverend McDermit smiled. 'Satan has desired to have you, that he may sift you as wheat.' Do you know who Jesus was talking to when he made that statement?"

Nathaniel thought for a moment. "Well, I would guess, ohhhh, more than likely, Judas, or one of the Pharisees."

"No, Jesus was talking to Peter. In fact he said it moments before Peter drew his sword and cut off the ear of the high priest who had come with a multitude to take Jesus away to be crucified. Peter was ready to take on an army in defense of Christ, yet it was at this point that the devil found him the most vulnerable! If we were to judge the situation by the circumstances and by what is right and wrong–these evil men taking away the Son of God to be tortured and murdered–Peter would seem to have had every right to run them all through with his sword. But Christ taught us that we also must let the Holy Spirit guide us, that his ways are higher than ours. Does this make sense to you Nathaniel?"

"Somewhat, but I am puzzled about one thing. How do you know for sure when you are doing the right thing–when it is time to fight and when it is time to lay down the sword?"

"You are still a babe in Christ; these things will take time. I have to confess that every once in a while I encounter situations when I am still not sure. Times will come in your life when you won't have the answer. You'll confront people and circumstances that will confound you, overwhelm you, threaten to swallow you up. When that time comes, there is one thing you must remember," Moses said, placing the can of paint on a shelf in the garage.

"What's that?" Nathaniel asked.

"Greater is he that is in you, than he that is in the world."

"That's it?" Nathaniel implored, somewhat disappointed.

"Yes, that's the core of it. You got that?"

"Yeah, sure, I guess so," he answered, though sounding not so sure.

"Good!" Moses announced, reaching into his pocket and handing something to Nathaniel. Nathaniel held it up and examined it. It was a key, an old tarnished skeleton key.

"Uh… thanks, Reverend McDermit," mumbled Nathaniel who hadn't the foggiest idea why Moses would give him such a thing.

Moses frowned, "Look at it closer, Nathaniel, look closer!"

Nathaniel held the key up and examined it. There, on one side of the key, he could see an inscription. It was almost worn off and was very small, but Nathaniel could still make it out. Nathaniel read it out loud: Greater is he that is in me,

"Turn it around, Nathaniel," Moses instructed anxiously, his eyes shining Nathaniel did and read that out loud. than he that is in the world. 1st John 4:4

"I had that made up for myself years and years ago so I would never forget it. I discovered that the verse, if followed, was the key to having a successful walk with God. The fellow who did the inscription for me sure gave me a funny look when I handed that key to him and asked him to try to put that scripture on it. Whenever I have felt forsaken or oppressed, I've reached into my pocket and felt that key, and then I remember. As you can see, I've almost rubbed the inscription off," he said chuckling. "I want you to have it, and whenever you find yourself doubting or in trouble, hopefully this key will remind you, too."

Nathaniel thanked him and put the key on his key chain. While he appreciated Moses' story and the reason behind it, the key meant more to him as a personal memento of Reverend McDermit.

"Well, that's about it. I think were done," Moses declared. "How about a nice big piece of pie and a cup of coffee? Oh, and remind me to open the windows and let some fresh air in. You never know how many days like this we'll have before winter sets in," Moses said as he pulled the garage door shut.

Moses and Nathaniel were just finishing up their second piece of pie and starting on their second pot of coffee when they heard a knock on the back door. "Hey, anybody home?" Reverend Fitch shouted, his head poking through the open back door.

Moses, who was seated with his back to the door, turned in his chair and shouted back, "Come in, Reverend, come on in!"

"Oh, I'm sorry, I didn't know you had company," Reverend Fitch said as he entered the kitchen.

Nathaniel stood up and held out his hand "Don't mind me, Reverend Fitch. I'm just here helping Reverend McDermit with a few odd jobs around the house."

Reverend Fitch grabbed Nathaniel's hand firmly, but never made eye contact as he continued to talk to Reverend McDermit. "I need to talk to you about something I've come across for our outreach program. It's the most exciting thing that I have ever seen!" he exclaimed dramatically, putting his briefcase on the table and popping the locks open.

Nathaniel immediately took a step forward, anxiously waiting to see the wonderful thing Reverend Fitch was so excited about.

At that same moment, Reverend Fitch, with his back to Nathaniel, looked over his shoulder and said "I'm sorry, son, this is something I need to talk to Reverend McDermit about—alone."

Reverend Fitch then turned toward Nathaniel, placed his hands on Nathaniel's shoulders, squeezed them, and said, "I'm sure you can find a few more odd jobs around the house. I won't be long." He gave

Nathaniel a pat on the back, exclaimed, "You're a good man!" and turned his back on Nathaniel again to attend to his briefcase.

"Oh… sure," Nathaniel responded quietly as he turned and walked toward the back door. "I need to finish cleaning up in the garage anyway."

As Nathaniel opened the back door and began walking toward the garage, he tried to ignore the nagging voice inside of him. "Can you believe that guy! He comes in out of nowhere, and with a pat on the back sends you out of the room like a child! Who does he think he is?" he grumbled to himself as he began to breathe faster and faster. "Slow down, Nathaniel, slow down," he voiced out loud to himself. "Remember what you and Reverend McDermit were just talking about. What just happened was nothing to get upset about. I'm sure that what Reverend Fitch had to show Reverend McDermit was something that he was not ready to show anyone in the congregation yet. It's in the planning stage. Don't take things so personally."

He paused at the garage door, took a deep breath, and slowly blew it out. "There, I'm feeling better already!" he thought as he gave the garage door a yank upward. "I still don't like the way he went about it," a small voice shouted back from inside him.

Back inside the house, Charlie Fitch was already deep into his presentation. "So you see, Reverend McDermit, by placing these ads strategically on the radio and on television, these studies prove that we could improve attendance at our church by an average of ten to twenty percent in the first year! In fact a church in Canton, Ohio, went from a congregation of two hundred fifty to over one thousand people in less than four years, and their demographics match ours almost exactly! Can you imagine that! One thousand people!"

"I don't mean to burst your bubble, Reverend Fitch," Moses calmly explained "but I've often wondered about something when it comes to churches of that size, a super church if you will. How are the needs of the individuals who attend such a church met? For example, how can a pastor take the time to counsel the couples with troubled marriages? And how do they build a close relationship with the youth of the church? I just can't see it. You know, Charlie, sometimes a pastor is all that stands in the way of a teenager and some bad choices that can haunt him the rest of his life. Why I remember Eddie Farrell—he's a pastor now, but when he was a teenager…"

"I appreciate your concerns, Reverend McDermit, I really, really, do," Reverend Fitch argued, interrupting Moses in mid sentence, "but aren't we missing the big picture here? Since every soul is precious in God's sight and needs to be saved, it is our commission to go to the four corners of the world to bring them in. We need to take advantage of such a wonderful tool that God has allowed us to have!" he exclaimed as he held up his briefcase. "We need to use every resource that is available to us!"

For a moment, all that could be heard was the ticking of the grandfather clock in the hall. Moses sat in his chair like a statue, his eyes fixed on the briefcase. He had always had the reputation of being somewhat of a stone-face, impossible to read.

"I wonder, Charlie," he finally said, "do all these facts and figures tell you how well these churches were ministering to the needs of all those people? Does it tell you what percent are still living for God a few years down the line? How about the pregnancy rate or drug use among its youth? I've guided this church through some pretty turbulent times—it was no picnic; many churches fell apart. Oh, I've lost a few church members; you always will. But on the whole I feel that by being available to every member of this congregation, I've had an impact on where they are today. Remember, God is not impressed with numbers. He values quality over quantity. I'm sure there are large churches out there that do a marvelous job. I'm not against having a large church if God wills it. But I'm also not comfortable with a church being superficially built up, a church built with gimmicks and mirrors. It won't last. It bothers me too much to see what happens to the people in these congregations when they come crashing down."

It was becoming obvious that Reverend Fitch was becoming irritated by this unexpected obstacle and was in no mood to listen. His face was becoming tense, the muscles on his jaw line began to roll, and he began to blink quickly as he talked.

"Reverend McDermit, I know that sometimes new ways are diffi-cult to accept and adjust to, but it is something that we as a church need to investigate. We have reached a point in the life of our church where it's time to move forward," he said, forcing a smile across his face. "We are standing at the edge of something great—I can feel it. I believe that we are this close," he asserted, holding his fingers a half-inch apart, "to having a great revival, one that could shake this city, this state, this country!" His voice was becoming more confident now.

"We have something special here. My wife and I felt it the moment we first stepped in this church. You have done a great work here, Moses, but it's time to reap the benefits of your labor. What do you say we give this a test run?" he implored as he held up the briefcase one more time. "I have faith that if you will just go over some of this with me, you will become just as excited as I am! Wait until you see this!" he announced as he started to take a fancy looking folder from the briefcase.

"Charlie, Charlie, you've become way too wrapped up in this," Moses stated with a smile on his face as he shook his head back and forth. "I've got to tell you that this isn't anything new! Let me ask you something. Have you ever heard of Aimee Semple McPhearson?"

"I guess, but I really don't see what she has to do with what we were talking about. Now I have…"

"Now wait a minute, Charlie, I wasn't finished. In the 1930s and 40s, she and others like her were among the first to capitalize on using the electronic and newspaper media to build churches whose atten-dance might reach thirty to forty thousand on any given Sunday morn-ing. They used to have to rent auditoriums to hold all the people that came to see them. Well, she eventually was involved in scandals that made headlines in every newspaper in the country. It was a real black eye on the ministry, and it was years before people forgot about it. Not too far back we had scandals involving those television evangelists. You yourself saw how it became a good excuse for every talk-show host and comedienne in the country to mock Christianity and its followers. It didn't matter to them that ninety-nine percent were good, honest people. I just don't think it's a real good way to build a church."

"So, you're telling me that there is no way you would ever consider these marketing techniques that I showed you?" Reverend Fitch asked.

"I'd have to say that's right. I'm sorry, I just don't feel good about that kind of thing; I never have. Don't worry, we will do all right, you wait and see. Now why don't you sit down and have a piece of pie, and I'll get you a cup of coffee."

"No thanks, Reverend McDermit. I think I really need to be going," Reverend Fitch replied as he gathered his papers together.

"I hope you're not too disappointed, Reverend Fitch. I understand your enthusiasm, and I know that your intentions are good…"

"I'll be okay., really. Well, I'll see you in church," he sharply responded as he quickly walked to the back door. Moses followed and watched as Reverend Fitch walked down the sidewalk to his car.

Within a few minutes Nathaniel came back in. "I heard Reverend Fitch pull out. Did you two get everything straightened out?"

"Oh, I think so. I may have ruffled his feathers a little, but he's a good man; it won't be long and he'll get over it."

CHAPTER FOUR

A Change in the Wind

L ittle did Moses know that something had changed on that sunny Wednesday afternoon, and in a way that would dramatically affect the rest of his life.

Before the church service the next Sunday morning, Moses arrived early, before morning's light, as he always did, to pray and go over his Sunday morning sermon in his office. He did this to be all alone in the church. But before going to his office in the back, Moses would first take a seat in the front row where the congregation sits. He would just sit there for a while, gazing at the pulpit, as though he were listening to a sermon being preached. Soon he would be quietly whispering, "Yes, Lord. Bless your name," a half dozen times or more as he nodded his head up and down.

There were two reasons he did this every Sunday morning. The first was to remind himself that no matter how high and mighty he might start to think that Reverend Moses McDermit was, it was still God's church. God was the one in charge, and he loved Reverend Moses McDermit no more than anyone else. The second reason was that Reverend McDermit wanted to listen to God's sermon before he preached his own that morning. He knew no better place than sitting in that big empty church where he was the only one listening.

Of course Moses heard no literal words coming down from the Almighty, but it was the spirit that preached to him, talked to his soul.

When he felt that God was finished with him this particular morning, Moses slowly pulled himself up to his feet and made his way to the back of the church.

As he neared his office, he thought that he could hear the muffled sounds of people talking. He paused for a moment and looked around. Seeing no one, he continued on for a few more steps, and then noticed light coming from underneath the door of an office just down the hall. It was Charlie Fitch's office.

He walked up to the door with a puzzled look on his face. His first thought was that Reverend Fitch had probably forgotten to turn off the light and left his radio on. But as he grew nearer, he could tell that it was no radio. Yes, there was definitely someone in the room, but Moses hadn't noticed any cars in the parking lot. Then another thought flashed through his mind. Was it possible that someone had broken into the church? Why, he thought, would anyone do that? He cocked his head toward the door and listened.

He could only pick out a few words here and there, because of the hushed tones. "Well, something needs to be done," he heard one voice say, and then more muffled voices.

"It's a difficult situation" he heard a voice closer to the door state. He heard another indiscernible comment and then some laughter.

"In the Lord's time, in the Lord's good time, fellahs!" Charlie Fitch's voice suddenly boomed out loud and familiar from the other side of the door.

"C'mon guys, it's got to be getting really late. We positively have to get going. I can't believe we've stayed here this long! Hey, Bud, what time do you have anyway?" Reverend Fitch shouted over his shoulder as he was opening the door.

"About five-thirty." Moses said as Charlie Fitch suddenly found himself standing face to face with Moses.

Charlie's bloodshot eyes suddenly grew large and round and all the color drained from his face. Four startled men behind him had similar expressions. "P-P-P-Pastor McDermit… you, you really gave me a scare!" he gasped, holding his right hand over his heart. "How long have you been standing there?"

Moses didn't say a word. He just stood there looking at the five of them. The four men that were still in the room appeared as if they were looking for some place to hide among the half-empty coffee cups and pizza boxes that littered the room.

"Oh, I just got here, Charlie. What are you men here for, an early prayer meeting?" Moses inquired.

Charlie studied Moses' face for a moment, as if he were trying to find something.

"Oh no, oh no!" he responded with a chuckle, adjusting his tie as he began to regain his composure.

He studied Moses' face again for an instant before he began again. "Is it really five-thirty!? Unbelievable! I guess we really let the time slip away from us, didn't we! I feel terrible about this!" he exclaimed, turning to look at the men in the room. They all stood there shaking their heads as if they too were amazed at their circumstance.

"You were saying," reminded Moses.

"Yes… as I was saying, I was here last evening, all alone, studying, when Bud Masterson walked in with Kirk, Matt, and Clay. Before we knew it, we started having a Bible study, and well, we must have lost all track of time! Five-thirty! I feel terrible about this!" he reiterated, shaking his head back and forth, smiling, but also trying to look properly repentant for his sin.

"Must have been a good Bible study, men," Moses commented, looking past Reverend Fitch and into the room. "Sorry I missed it! What was it about?"

The four men began looking at each other, hemming and hawing, each one waiting for the other to speak.

"I think we just about covered the gambit, Reverend McDermit!" Charlie quickly spoke up. "It just sort of evolved into a lot of different topics. You know how that is. You always have that Daniel fellah asking you a hundred and one questions."

"Nathaniel," Moses said.

"What?" Charlie replied.

"Nathaniel O'Brien."

Reverend Fitch's face went blank for a second.

"Ohhhhh, right, you mean the fellah that I had just mentioned. Right, Nathaniel."

An awkward pause followed.

"Well, Pastor McDermit, it is awfully late... er... early," Fitch said with a chuckle.

"We should be getting home. Sorry if we bothered you this morning," Bud said as he and the other three men quickly filed out of the room past Moses.

"How would you men be getting home? I mean, I didn't see any cars in the lot?" Moses queried.

"Oh... wel-l-l... we were having coffee just down the road at the Big Bear restaurant, and it being such a nice fall evening, we all decided to walk up to the church," Bud responded, seeming a little nervous.

"That's a pretty good walk. What is it, about a mile and a half, two miles?" Moses asked.

"It couldn't be that far, could it?" Bud disputed out loud as the others looked puzzled, as if trying to estimate the exact distance in their heads.

"However far it is, I'll be needing to catch a ride with you since my wife dropped me off here. She was driving up to that ministers' wives' conference up in Taylor's Falls and staying the night," Charlie responded as he closed the door to his office.

"Well, then how had you originally planned to get home, Charlie?" Moses asked.

"Oh... I thought I'd just grab a cab," he replied slowly. "We better get going, Reverend McDermit. I'll need to freshen up before church."

The five men began making their way toward the back door at the rear of the church.

"Hey..." Moses yelled out.

"Yes sir?" Charlie answered, turning his head over his shoulder as he walked.

"Be careful, my friends."

An uneasiness settled on Charlie's face as he suddenly stopped and turned around.

"You've all been up all night, be careful when you drive home," Moses added as he looked at Charlie with his wise old eyes.

"Oh… yeah… of course we will," he mumbled as he took a couple steps backward, gazing back into the old man's eyes. He then turned and walked out the door.

Moses watched as the door slowly closed behind them. Of course, he had a very good idea of what went on in Charlie Fitch's office last night. Twenty years ago he would have handled the situation much differently. Reverend Fitch would have been loading up his belongings in boxes right now. But age and a lifetime had mellowed Moses, and he soon emptied his mind of it and went into his office to study for that morning's sermon.

Reverend Fitch arrived at the morning service a little blurry-eyed, but still able to pump life into the congregation as he led the song service. Moses' preaching, as usual, was solid and uplifting. Reverend Fitch appeared a little nervous as the service ended, perhaps waiting for the other shoe to drop. Moses approached him as the congregation was being dismissed and gave him a big pat on the back. Anyone who knew Moses well at all knew that that was his way of telling you everything was going to be all right. "Let's go greet the people," was all he said.

The two men stood on opposite sides of the front steps of the church, shaking hands with the congregation, complimenting the women on their clothing and children, ribbing the men good-naturedly about their weight or thinning hair; a scene played out thousands of times every Sunday morning in churches across America.

Nathaniel made his way up to Moses, waiting behind two elderly women who were giving him every detail of their latest bursitis attacks. They finally moved on and Nathaniel stepped forward, extending his hand.

"Good morning, Pastor, I…" before Nathaniel could finish, he felt Moses' left hand grasp his right forearm tightly.

"Help me inside!" Moses gasped.

Startled, Nathaniel's eyes quickly went from his forearm to Moses' face. It appeared very pale, and he could see pain etched in his eyes. He could feel Moses' body trembling.

"I need help, I feel sick and I'm having trouble moving my right leg. I think I'm having a stroke!" Moses gasped again.

"I'll have someone call an ambulance," Nathaniel stated, trying to comfort him.

"No! Don't you dare do that! Just help me inside and don't cause a scene!"

It was against Nathaniel's better judgment, but he thought at this moment it was better not to upset the pastor. Moses clung tightly to his arm and slowly shuffled back into the church. It was all but empty, and Nathaniel helped him sit down in the first available pew.

"Bring your truck around to the front of the church, Nathaniel," Moses whispered.

"No, Reverend McDermit! I need to call an ambulance now! You're in no shape to walk out to my truck! If you think you're having a stroke…"

"Listen," Moses explained slowly but forcefully, "I don't want the church to see me wheeled out on a stretcher, with an oxygen mask strapped to my face. Just pull your truck up and let's go."

Nathaniel could tell by the look in the older man's eyes that he meant business. Nathaniel was concerned that if he argued any more, Reverend McDermit would try to get up and drive himself, no matter how remote the chances were that he would even make it to his car.

"Okay, okay. I'll get my truck!" Nathaniel stammered as he dashed for the door, doubt flooding his mind on whether or not he was doing the right thing.

He raced to the parking lot and pulled his pickup up to the front of the church. He ran back up the sidewalk, up the seven cement steps and back into the church, where he found Reverend Fitch approaching Moses.

"Yes sir, yes sir, what a fine morning, Pastor McDermit!" he announced in his southern drawl. "The spirit of God was surely here this morning. Did you see the looks on the faces of the people as we greeted them? Good service! Good Service! What a fine morning too, I…"

"Excuse me, Reverend Fitch, Pastor McDermit isn't feeling well, and…" Nathaniel interrupted, putting himself between the two men.

"Hold on there, son, I'm talking to the pastor now," Reverend Fitch cut in, a scowl on his face. "You'll just have to wait and talk to him later, especially if he's not feeling well. There's a time and place for…"

"I think he's having a stroke!" Nathaniel tersely stated, speaking through clenched teeth. "Help me get him out to my truck!"

"Wh-wh-wh-what? A stroke!" The color dropped from his face and a look of panic seemed to envelop him. "Are you sure?" he questioned, looking at Nathaniel and then looking down at Moses, who was now resting his head on the pew in front of him.

"Help me get him out to my truck. The sooner we can get him to the hospital the better."

"Shouldn't we be calling 911? I mean, I don't think this is a good idea!" he exclaimed, alarm in his voice.

"He wouldn't let me. Now help me get him to his feet."

The two men grabbed Moses under the arms and lifted him upright. "We're going to walk towards the door now," Nathaniel instructed Moses, who opened and closed his eyes in acknowledgment.

They slowly made their way to the front door. They went out of the building and stood at the top of the cement steps. There were about fifteen to twenty people still standing about, conversing. Step by step the three men began to make their way down to the sidewalk.

The people gradually became aware that something was wrong. Their discussions stopped in mid sentence as they turned to watch the men make their way down the steps.

One of the ushers jogged up as they reached the bottom of the steps. "Is everything all right, Pastor McDermit?" he asked.

To Nathaniel's astonishment, he felt Moses shake himself loose from their grasp and pull himself fully erect. "I'm fine, Jack, just a little dizzy."

"Everything's all right," Moses announced to the people that began to gather around him. "I'm all right. You can all go home."

The people slowly began to disperse. Nathaniel and Reverend Fitch again began walking Moses to the car. When they were a few feet from the truck, Nathaniel let go of Moses and opened the front door directly in front of him. Moses, who now had beads of sweat covering his forehead, stepped forward with the help of Charlie Fitch, bent over, and collapsed into the seat.

"What should I do now?" Charlie nervously asked.

Nathaniel shut the passenger door and ran around to the driver's side. "You can meet me at St. Andrew's Hospital. I might need some help there!" he responded as he jumped into the truck.

It was only a twenty-minute drive to the hospital, but to Nathaniel it seemed to last forever. He looked over at Moses, who was slumped up against the door, eyes closed, his left hand held up against the side of his face. Nathaniel was afraid to even ask Moses if he was all right, fearing the energy expended just to answer back would weaken him all the more.

The hospital finally came into view and Nathaniel pulled his truck into the emergency lot. Reverend Fitch was nowhere to be found, so Nathaniel ran inside and explained the circumstances. Two staff members came back out with him and hurried Moses into the hospital in a wheelchair. Charlie Fitch showed up forty-five minutes later, explaining that he had gone to the wrong hospital. He ended his explanation with "Bless your heart, son, but you'll have to speak more clearly. With your directions I ended up doing a whole lot of running around!"

Moses was diagnosed as having had a moderate stroke that left his right arm and right leg slightly paralyzed. He spent the next few weeks in the hospital recuperating and in physical therapy.

The church members flooded his room with plants and flowers. Reverend Fitch, of course, became acting pastor, dramatically retelling the story of the incident at the very next service. In his version, however, Nathaniel was omitted by name except for a reference to "the fine help some of the saints gave me during that time of tragedy."

"We're so lucky you were here, Reverend. What a blessing you and your wife have become to this church. Pastor McDermit is so lucky that you just happened to be there, that you came along at just the right time. Who knows what might have happened to him if you hadn't?" Nathaniel heard this and similar comments from the congregation as admirers gathered around Reverend Fitch after church services.

Nathaniel winced when he heard talk like this. It wasn't because he was jealous or wanted any glory for himself, but it was because of the way Reverend Fitch never clarified what actually happened and seemed to be using Moses' stroke to his own advantage. To Nathaniel, it appeared to be quite manipulative on Reverend Fitch's part. At any rate, for whatever reason he was doing it, it appeared to be working, Nathaniel thought. Besides having an engaging and charismatic personality, Reverend Fitch had now made himself an instant hero and seemed to be carefully cultivating and nurturing that image.

As the weeks went by, the church became utterly fascinated by Reverend Fitch and his wife, and even Nathaniel had to admit he had never heard such preaching and singing in his life. The congregation seemed to be exploding with energy.

Nathaniel stopped almost daily to see Moses, who had come home. When asked how the services were going, Nathaniel assured him that everything was going running smoothly.

Moses was making remarkable progress. Only two months had gone by since the stroke and he was already making it around the house with a walker. Nathaniel stopped by one Sunday afternoon on his way home from church. It seemed like old times, with the two men sitting at the kitchen table, drinking their customary cups of coffee.

"I seem to be getting stronger every day, Nathaniel. Give me another week or two and I'll be back behind the pulpit!" he proudly stated.

Although Nathaniel felt it would be best if Moses returned as soon as possible, he also was concerned that he was pushing things too fast.

"Don't rush yourself, Pastor. You need to fully recuperate before you even think about returning to your pastoral duties. A stroke isn't like a cold or the flu. You have to give your body time to heal itself. The church will be there when you're ready to come back, but you've earned some time off."

Moses grimaced. "My life—your life, everybody's life is a vapor. One minute we are here, the next we're gone. You know something, if I didn't know any better, I'd say it was just a few years ago that I came here to Lexington with a young wife and children."

Moses closed his eyes. "I can still see the trolley cars traveling up and down the tracks as I drove through the city for the first time. I can still hear my children arguing in the back seat. I think they were fighting over some dancing wooden toy. I can even smell the smells of the city that day!" he exclaimed.

He opened his eyes. "But that was over forty years ago! Over forty years! Nathaniel, that may sound like a long time to you, but it went by like that!" he said snapping his fingers. "'Whereas ye know not what shall be on the morrow. For what is your life? It is even a vapor, that appeareth for a little time, and then vanisheth away,'" Moses quoted. "Book of James. And it's so true, Nathaniel, so true! So you see, we have no time to rest. We have so little time as it is!"

Nathaniel could see the joy and excitement in Moses' eyes. "Amazing," Nathaniel thought to himself. "This man literally lives and breathes the gospel."

Nathaniel stood up. "It's getting late, I'd better be going," he said, squeezing Moses' shoulder.

"You can tell anyone who asks that I'll be back preaching before they know it, maybe in a week, two weeks at the latest," he stated confidently, patting Nathaniel on the back. "I'll have to schedule a meeting with the church board so they can fill me in on what's been going on and our plans for this spring. Maybe we'll plan a revival, bring in an evangelist. What do you think?" he asked with a smile on his face and a twinkle in his eye.

"Sounds great, Pastor," replied Nathaniel, amused at the grit and desire Moses displayed. "It will be good to have you back."

Nathaniel threw on his coat and stepped out into the frigid winter air. The days were short, and the sun was just a mellow glow in the western sky. He hopped in his truck and headed for home, which was only a few miles away. It was early January, and it was bitterly cold. He was lucky if the cab in his truck was warm by the time he pulled into his driveway. He shivered and reached for the knob on the radio. He listened for a few moments to some music, decided it wasn't to his liking and punched a button. A deep-voiced talk-show host was interviewing a woman who claimed to have been Julius Caesar in one of her past lives.

Nathaniel rolled his eyes and punched another button. A woman with a beautiful voice was singing a gospel song. "Pretty voice," Nathaniel thought to himself. "Almost sounds like Jennifer Fitch."

"Hello, friends," a male voice broke in as the music faded. "Have the troubles of this world weighed you down so much that you barely have the strength to get out of bed in the morning? Do drugs, alcohol, or gambling have you tightly in their grasp? Folks, I wish you'd join us at Mount Calvary Church in Lexington for a time of renewal and fellowship. We have a wonderful attended nursery for the younger children and Sunday school classes for the older ones. This is Reverend Charles Fitch, inviting you to worship with us this Sunday morning. For more information call 651-229-HELP, that's 651-229-4357. Thank you, and we are looking forward to seeing you this Sunday morning!"

CHAPTER FIVE

A Storm is Brewing

"Hello, you have reached Mount Calvary Church! Our services are held on Thursdays at seven o' clock p.m., and on Sunday mornings at ten o' clock. Sunday's evening service begins at seven o' clock. If you need directions or have any questions, please stay on the line, and our friendly staff will assist you. Thank you for calling Mount Calvary Church!"

Click, click.

"Hello, this is Mount Calvary Church! How may I help you?" answered a perky female voice.

"Yes, I'd like to speak to Reverend Fitch, please."

"I'm sorry, Reverend Fitch is not available at this time. May I help you?"

"You certainly can," a gruff voice shot back. "This is Reverend Moses McDermit, pastor of Mount Calvary Church. You can tell Reverend Charles Fitch to call me immediately! …By the way, who is this?"

"Ohhhh… ah… hello, Pastor McDermit. This is Missy Anderson. Um… how are you feeling?"

"Missy Anderson! What in the world! It's Monday morning. Why aren't you school?"

"Pastor McDermit, don't you remember? I graduated last spring! Reverend Fitch gave me this part-time job. Isn't it great!"

"Yes, yes, I'm sure it is," Moses responded trying to tone down the irritation in his voice. "Well if Reverend Fitch isn't there, where is he?"

"Oh, he's here all right. He just told me not to bother him unless it was, like, an emergency. Do you want me to connect you with him?"

"Connect me with him? What do you mean by that? Just go get him for me."

"Oh, I forgot. You probably don't know! We've had a new phone system installed. Isn't that excellent? Reverend Fitch has a new phone in his office and like all I have to do is press a button and you can talk to him."

"Please press the button, Missy."

"Great! Hold on, Pastor McDermit! Okay, let's see, whoops…" There was a click, a few moments of silence, and then a dial tone.

Moses shook his head, pursed his lips and redialed.

"Hello, you have reached Mount Calvary Church! Our services…" Moses more than firmly hung up the phone. That was enough for him. He slowly got to his feet, grabbed a newly bought cane, slapped his hat on his head and was out the door.

Meanwhile, back at the church, Charlie Fitch was in his office with Bud Masters, a member of the church board and one of the men who had been at the overnight "Bible study" in Charlie's office months earlier.

"It's going to be real interesting to see how many visitors we have here Thursday night, Bud. Of course, I think that the biggest response from the radio ad will be on a Sunday morning, because that's when most people traditionally go to church."

"You're probably right, Reverend Fitch. That would seem to make sense. Have we received any calls yet on the ad?" Bud questioned.

"I've got the Anderson girl sitting by the answering machine. She's keeping track of all the inquiries. The ad's only been on since last night so I wouldn't expect too much," Charlie remarked, reaching for his briefcase. He plopped it onto his desk and popped the locks.

"C'mere, Bud, let me show you the timetable on some of this stuff," he said with pride, pulling out a fancy folder bulging with impressive looking graphs and charts. It was the same literature that he had attempted to show Moses last autumn.

Barely able to contain the waves of excitement that rolled over him, Charlie excitedly began to look over all the multicolored charts with Bud.

There was a knock at the door. "Reverend Fitch? Reverend Fitch? Are you in there?"

"Yes, Missy, what do you need?" Charlie answered back through the closed door, annoyed that he had been stopped in the middle of his presentation, even though he had given Bud Masters the same presentation at least a half a dozen times before.

"I almost forgot to tell you. Pastor McDermit called about a half an hour ago. I tried to connect him with you, but I must have cut him off."

"Did he say what he wanted?"

"Well, like, not really. I don't think so."

"Thank you, Missy. Go back to the phone now."

A few minutes later there was another knock at the door.

"Reverend Fitch, someone wants to know if we are east or west of Schichel's Bakery on White Bear Avenue. I'm never quite sure on my directions, so like, I was afraid to say for sure."

"We're east, Missy, east! I thought we had this straightened out this morning!" Charlie grumbled back through the door.

"Well, you know, I just didn't want to give someone the wrong directions. So, you said it was east, right?"

"East, Missy, east!" Charlie snapped.

"Okay, thanks, Reverend Fitch!"

Charlie went back to his presentation, "Now Bud, before I forget, let me show you the most impressive..."

Knock, knock, knock went the door.

"Oh, for crying out loud!" Charlie grumbled. He slapped a chart onto the table, took four long quick strides to the door and flung it open. "Listen, Missss..." he said, stopping in midsentence. Reverend McDermit stood there, somber faced, clutching his hat in one hand, the other resting on his cane.

"Well, Pastor McDermit! What an unexpected surprise!" Charlie sputtered as he gathered himself together. He tried to pull the door closed behind him and maneuver around Moses.

"No need to come out. We'll talk in here," Moses stated flatly, pushing the door back open and making his way past Charlie.

Bud Masters was soon aware Reverend McDermit was outside the door and had positioned himself in a corner of the room so as not to be seen from the hallway. Moses glanced over at him, then at the graphs and charts on Charlie's desk, and then back to Bud Masters.

"Bud, if I didn't know any better, I'd say you were hiding back there."

"Oh! Of course not!" Bud blustered, stepping forward, his face glowing red with embarrassment. "I was just... I was... Ahhh..." But nothing would come to him.

"Never mind, Bud. Reverend Fitch and I are going to need some privacy. Would you mind too much..." he stated more than asked.

Bud said nothing as he quickly made his way out of the room. Even from behind one could still see his ears glowing an embarrassed bright red.

"Well, Moses, you seem to be in a rather serious mood. I hope nothing has happened. Are you and your family all right?" Charlie asked, standing in the doorway.

"Sit down, Charlie, and close the door behind you."

Charlie closed the door and walked over to his desk, quickly trying to gather up all the literature that he had dumped on it. "You'll have to excuse the mess. Just give me a moment and I'll clear this away."

"Forget it, Charlie. I've already seen it. I know what it is."

Charlie, realizing there wasn't much else he could say or do, gave a weak smile and sat down. Moses stood at the front of the desk. "I think what hurts most is that you did all this behind my back—when I was in the hospital!" he said shaking his head back and forth. "How in the world did you think I would never find out about this?" he questioned, holding up a pile of papers on Charlie's desk. "I can't quite figure that one out. Or maybe you just assumed I wasn't coming back. Was that it? You did all of this—the radio ads, the new phone system, Missy Anderson, and who knows what else without even consulting me! If you recall, I'm still the pastor here, you know. I thought we had settled this months ago! Can you explain any of this?"

"Of course I can. It's rather obvious, isn't it? You had a stroke and I was left in charge. With you in the hospital in your serious condition, I wasn't about to go running up there, disturbing you every time I had to make a decision," Charlie replied, self-righteousness creeping into his voice. "You know, I've shouldered a lot of the responsibility around here for what, five years now? Suddenly, you're gone and I'm in charge, yet I'm not in charge. What was I supposed to do?"

"Charlie, some of what you say is true. Yes, you have carried a lot of the workload around here, and you've done a good job. Maybe I haven't given you enough credit for that in the past. For that, I'll apologize. But there's something different about you. I guess I didn't want to see it at first. Maybe I didn't want to believe it, but you've changed. You're evasive and elusive, manipulative. This church, the ministry, seems to have become almost a game to you, a game you want to win at all costs," he explained, again holding up some of the papers on Charlie's desk.

"You say you had no choice but to take control and so you went ahead and implemented these programs while I was sick. But the truth is that we had discussed this program quite thoroughly at my house months ago. I gave you very good reasons why we shouldn't do it. But you were still set on doing it—somehow, someway. Tell me, Charlie. Wasn't that the real reason you had that all-night meeting in your office with Bud and the other men last fall?"

"What meeting are you talking about?" Charlie asked, with a look of puzzlement on his face. He paused for a moment as if probing his memory. "Oh-h-h-h yes, the time we forgot how late it was and had a Bible study until, what was it, five in the morning?" Charlie responded with a grin, shaking his head back and forth. "Well, let me think, that was a long time ago, Pastor. You know we talked about a lot of things that night. Now if I remember right…"

"Charlie."

"Hold on. It's coming to me…"

"Charlie!" Moses snapped. "Charlie, one of the men at your meeting came to me in the hospital and told me everything. I guess his conscience was bothering him. Even as I was driving over here I wasn't really sure what I was going to do about it, but now you've made up my mind for me. I'm going to have to let you go, Charlie. Quite frankly, I don't trust you anymore and I'm not comfortable with your attitude. I'm not sure if it's ambition that's driving you or something else, but I can't ignore it any more. I've got to have someone who shares my values and ideals. It's really a shame, because I had hoped that one day you would take over this church. Now it's clear to me that that never can be. You've meant a lot to this church and to me. I will always consider you my friend, but it's not going to work anymore. It's mid January. I wouldn't normally do this, but since you've been here so long, I'm giving you three months to find something else. That gives you until mid April."

Charlie Fitch looked completely dumbfounded. Clearly, he hadn't expected Moses to be so severe with him. "Wait a minute, Reverend McDermit," he protested, tears in his eyes. "I know I may have gotten a little carried away, but don't you think this is a little harsh! I mean, a little ad on the radio, some phone lines... Can't you give me another chance?"

"I'm sorry, Charlie, I've made up my mind." Moses turned and walked out the door.

Charlie Fitch folded his arms on top of the desk, buried his face in them, and began to weep bitterly. He then raised his head, glared at the empty doorway and said, "This isn't over yet, Reverend McDermit, not by a long shot!"

Moses decided he would return to the church services that Thursday, earlier than even he would have liked. He was still a little weak and wobbly. But after finding out about all the shenanigans Charlie Fitch had pulled while he was gone, he felt it prudent to return expeditiously. He decided not to tell the congregation about Reverend Fitch leaving until it was absolutely necessary. He wanted to give Charlie a chance to find another job and come to grips with the situation. It would also cut down on the time that rumors and gossip invariably spread about in a church in situations like this. No one ever needed to know the how's and why's of Reverend Fitch's leaving.

Thursday evening Moses received a standing ovation as he slowly made his way to the pulpit to thank the church members for their prayers, flowers, and cards. Charlie Fitch preached, and if one didn't know any better, one would think that everything was returning to normal. The relationship between the two men, though somewhat strained, seemed cordial as they began to work together again.

For a while things were uneventful, and, indeed, everything did seem to be returning to the way things had been. Oh, Missy Anderson was somewhat confused about why she was suddenly out of a job, but that soon passed as she was hired at a local supermarket serving fillet-o-fish samples to customers. There was less pressure and she seemed much happier.

And so it went, until one evening when Nathaniel was playing basketball with a group of men from church in the church cafeteria, which doubled as their gymnasium. After about forty-five minutes of spirited play, the men, who ranged in years from teen aged to middle-aged, called for a break. Sweaty and red-faced, they broke into groups of two or three, collapsing on to the floor with their backs against the wall, each attempting to catch his breath while engaging in small talk. Nathaniel made his way to the other side of the cafeteria to buy a drink out of the soda machine. When he returned, he overheard a conversation among a group of the younger men.

"Yeah, he had some radio ads planned, I guess a few of them even got on the air. Jason, didn't you say that you heard one?" Nathaniel overheard one of them say as he returned.

"Yeah, I heard it. It was a real good ad too. Reverend Fitch sounded smooth. But, from what I hear, for some reason or another, the old man wouldn't go for it," Jason answered with a smirk.

"Why not? I can't believe it! What could be wrong with something like that? You'd think he'd want to encourage that kind of thing!"

another one remarked in amazement.

"Don't you think that's a little disrespectful?" Nathaniel interrupted.

"What do you mean?" Jason asked as all three looked up at Nathaniel, who was standing near them holding a basketball.

"I mean the way you referred to Pastor McDermit as the "old man" and the tone of your voices. It sounded a little disrespectful to me."

"I don't know what you're talking about. I don't think any of us were talking like that. Chill out, man," Jason responded coolly. "Hey guys, let's play a quick game of PIG before we get started again," he said to the other two as he jumped to his feet. The three of them grabbed another ball and left.

Nathaniel barely had time to let any of it register when a side door suddenly burst open. "Hey, Reverend Fitch!" the group shouted.

"Hey, guys, sorry I'm late! I had some things I had to do, but I got here as soon as I could."

"What he really means is as soon as his wife lets him come," someone shouted.

"Shhhhhh," he whispered, holding a finger up to his puckered lips. "No one's supposed to know that!"

Everyone roared with laughter. Everyone except Nathaniel. With what he had just heard moments before, he felt uncomfortable about the whole situation. He set the ball down and walked out the back. No one noticed that he had left.

Though Nathaniel was somewhat of a loner, even he started picking up bits and pieces of gossip over the next few weeks, remarks and attitudes similar to the comments at the gym. For whether it was in the back corner of the lobby in church or when they bumped into each other at the supermarket, the church people began to talk. Little did Nathaniel know that a feeding frenzy had begun.

"Maybe Reverend McDermit has just gotten too old for the job. Maybe it's time he thought about retiring…"

"I heard that the stroke affected his mind, that he becomes confused about things. You know, a little senile. That poor old man. You've got to feel sorry for him, but still, if he's standing in God's way when he wants the church to grow, well…"

"What! Sarah, are you serious? What's that? You heard that Moses fired Reverend Fitch! Where did you hear that? You say he was jealous over those ads? Can you imagine that, and after Reverend Fitch saved his life. Well, that's a shame, and after all the fine years that Reverend McDermit has had here, to do something like that. What's that? You heard the stroke is muddling up his thinking? Well, that explains it…"

"All I know, Tom, is that when Reverend Fitch is up there preaching, something special happens. He's been anointed by God. As far as I am concerned, Reverend Fitch has been every bit the pastor Reverend McDermit has. Moses is in for a big surprise if he thinks he can just remove this man of God. To be honest with you, McDermit's always been a little too bossy and self-righteous for me anyway. He's standing in the way of growth and that's not scriptural…"

"You say Pastor McDermit is going to let Reverend Fitch go? All because Reverend Fitch wanted to start a program to reach the lost? You know, I don't think that's right, not right at all! Something has got to be done. Someone has to do something!"

As the rumors and innuendoes grew, things began to change in the once model church. Moses, who regularly preached every Sunday morning, began to notice a drop-off in attendance for that service. It also seemed that some of the congregation was avoiding him when he greeted them after church.

Word finally reached Moses from two long-time friends about the gossip that was now starting to spread like a fire out of control. Moses had a very good idea of the source.

"Say, Charlie, will you come into my office? There are a few things that I need to discuss with you," Moses called out to Charlie as he walked past Moses' office.

"I'm sorry I'm pretty busy right now. Can it wait?" he stated more than asked.

"No, I don't think so. I'd appreciate it if you stepped into my office for a few moments."

It was hardly noticeable, but a smirk flashed across Charlie's face as he hesitated for a moment and went in the office.

"Sit down, Charlie," said Moses, who was sitting at his big oak desk. Charlie sat down across from him. "I'd like us to pray before we start. Is that all right with you?" Moses asked.

"Oh, ah, sure, fine," Charlie mumbled.

"Dear Father, we ask you to be here with us in this room to guide our thoughts and our words. We ask you to help us direct our conversation in a way that will be pleasing to you. Help both of us to remain friends, even though our lives may end up taking different paths. We ask this in Jesus' name. Amen."

"Amen," Charlie repeated, appearing somewhat uncomfortable.

"Charlie, I've asked you in here because I've been told that the congregation is talking about the two of us. It's being said that I'm jealous of you and because of that I've been interfering with God's will. I've even heard that I'm just a confused old man, mentally disabled from my stroke," Moses said with a wry grin.

"And now I hear," Moses said, leaning forward onto his desk "that it is for the reasons I've just mentioned, that I'm letting you go. I'm wondering, do you know anything about this?"

"Why should I know anything about it?" Charlie replied impassively.

"Well, since I know that I haven't told anyone about a private conversation that went on between the two of us, I thought that logically you would be the person to ask."

Charlie said nothing for a moment, his eyes wandering the room, and his hand drumming the front of the desk. "Yeah. I know something about it," he suddenly replied quite brazenly. "Did you really think you were going to keep it a secret?"

"A secret? What are you talking about?"

"I mean, really, did you think I was just going to go quietly into the night without a whimper? We can't make you look bad, can we? We'll wait a week or so before ol' Charlie leaves, then we'll tell the congregation so things don't get too hot. He'll be gone and they'll forget about him. Well, let me tell you something. I won't let you do this to them Pastor, not this time. You may have done it to others, but not me. I won't be your sacrificial lamb!"

Moses was caught almost completely off guard. He had thought that he knew Charlie quite well by now. He had expected evasiveness from him or some type of excuse, no matter how implausible. What he hadn't expected was such an open defiance, and how he spoke as though he were fighting for some holy and noble cause. "I won't let you do this to "them" and "sacrificial lamb" rang in Moses' ears.

"Charlie," Moses said calmly "I didn't want to tell the congregation about your leaving right away because I felt that by waiting there would be less time for speculating about why you were leaving. Did you want me to stand up in the next service and say 'Reverend Fitch is leaving us because he broke an agreement that we had made and did it while I was in the hospital recovering from my stroke?' That wouldn't have done you or them any good. Maybe it wasn't the best way to handle it, but it's the best way I could come up with. If I've offended you, I'm truly sorry. I didn't mean to."

Charlie rose to his feet. "That's fine. You can apologize, but I'm afraid I can't let it go that easily. You see, I've got these people to think about. I've got the souls in this city to think about. I accept your apology, I hope it was sincere. It's a start for you. I only hope you can repent from all the other wounds you have inflicted among so many in this church," he lectured as he went toward the door.

"I think I know what you're going to try and do, Charlie. Don't do it. For your own sake and the congregation's. Please don't do this."

Charlie smirked, shook his head and walked out the door.

Things soon went from bad to worse. Charlie quit speaking to Moses, cooperating with him only to get through a church service. It was now mid-March, and even though Charlie Fitch would be gone in a few weeks, the situation had escalated to a point that Moses soon realized he could no longer wait until April. He was concerned about the effect this was having on the people in the congregation. Reluctant as he was, he called Charlie back into his office to tell him he would have to leave as soon as possible, no later than the end of the week.

"That's all fine and good, Reverend McDermit," Charlie responded curtly, "but have you discussed this with the church board? If you recall, we are living in a democracy and you do need their approval."

"I've never had any trouble with the church board," Moses replied.

"You've never tried to fire an assistant pastor," Charlie dryly answered.

Moses didn't like the tone of Charlie's voice. It was too confident, almost mocking. "Fine, Charlie, have it your way. I'll call a board meeting—tonight if possible."

"I'll be there," Charlie said aloofly, seemingly unconcerned.

After many phone calls, a hastily called meeting was scheduled for that evening.

Moses sat at one end of the table as the nine men on the board arrived and made their way one by one into the church conference room. They all looked very uncomfortable, for they well knew what this meeting was about. Charlie Fitch was the last to arrive. He entered with his usual dramatic flair, looking tall, handsome, and polished, briefcase in hand.

Moses opened the meeting in prayer. He again spelled out why they were there, and with a short explanation, told the board why he felt it was necessary that Reverend Fitch be removed from his position of assistant pastor as soon as possible. Many of the faces on the board registered surprise when they heard Moses' account of the story; it certainly differed from the one that had been making its way around the church. Reverend Fitch then was given his chance to reply. He responded in a way that only he could, playing to emotion, weaving together a story that Aesop himself would envy and tying it up with a neat bow at the end. It was a masterful job. The board questioned both men for approximately forty-five minutes and then the board chairman, Marvin Olafson, called for a ballot vote.

The ballots were quickly tallied, and Marvin Olafson self-consciously stood to announce the results. "Ahhhheeeemmmmm…" he nervously cleared his throat "let the record show that there were two votes, ahhhhhh…" he said in a shaky voice, clearing his throat again, "two votes in favor of relieving Reverend Charles Fitch of his ministerial duties at Mount Calvary Church and seven votes to retain Reverend Charles Fitch. It is therefore the recommendation of this board that Reverend Charles Fitch remain at Mount Calvary as its assistant pastor."

Before the words were barely out of Marvin Olafson's mouth, Bud Masters quickly stood up and read from a prepared statement. "Because of the turmoil that has surrounded this church since last fall and continues to this day, a lack of confidence has developed in the congregation concerning its active pastor, Reverend Moses McDermit. Many have expressed concern about his health and also the direction that their church is headed. While many have indicated there is a deep appreciation and respect for his many years of service, they also feel that their concerns can no longer be ignored and must be addressed. With all due respect, I move that a vote be expeditiously taken among board members to recommend that the church be allowed to vote on whether or not to retain Reverend Moses McDermit as pastor of Mount Calvary Church." Bud sat down, never lifting his eyes from the prepared statement.

"I second the motion," another board member quickly added.

"What in the world is going on here. What did you just say, Bud?" one of the older board members asked.

"In laymen's terms, he wants you men to open my job up to a church vote, Jack!" Moses said tersely, casting a steely gaze at Bud, who wouldn't raise his eyes to meet it.

The room erupted with noise and debate, and only abated when Marvin Olafson began to bang his coffee cup loudly on the table. "This meeting will come to order!" he shouted. "We will have order!"

"Whether you agree or disagree with what was just said," Marvin continued, "the rules now require we take a vote on the motion."

The ballots were soon readied. Moses looked down at the other end of the table at Charlie, who appeared relaxed and unperturbed.

One by one the nine men returned their folded pieces of paper to Marvin Olafson.

CHAPTER SIX

Gone

Marvin stood for the second time that evening to read the results, "By a five to four vote this board has chosen to recommend that a vote be taken by the church body on whether Reverend Moses McDermit should continue as pastor of Mount Calvary Church."

Marvin Olafson announced at the conclusion of the next church service that a special business meeting would be held on Saturday, April 1, at 7 p.m., and that a vote would be taken at that time on whether Reverend Moses McDermit would continue as pastor of Mount Calvary Church. There were gasps of shock from some members of the congregation, followed by noisy whispering. Marvin then dismissed the congregation and they silently made their way down the aisles and out to their cars.

Nathaniel ran up to Moses after the service, stunned and angered by the announcement. "Reverend McDermit, what's going on here? Why have they called for a vote on whether to keep you as our pastor?" he asked angrily.

Moses smiled and patted Nathaniel on the shoulder.

"Don't worry my friend; everything's all right; keep your sword in its sheath."

"Its Charlie Fitch, isn't it? He's behind this; a blind man could see it! What a brave man he is, hiding behind his smooth talk and fancy schemes! Someone should…"

"Nathaniel!" Moses shouted, his eyes on fire. "How dare you talk like that in God's house! I thought I'd taught you better than that! Whether you like Reverend Fitch or not, he's still a minister and if he's done wrong, believe you me, it will catch up with him sooner or later! Nathaniel, don't disappoint me now. I have enough on my mind as it is."

Nathaniel suddenly felt very small and foolish. He didn't totally understand or agree with Moses' logic, but it was apparent that he had upset the pastor. The whole situation was leaving Nathaniel feeling very confused about many things. Reverend McDermit, the ministry, Christianity, and the behavior of people who profess to be its followers. Emotion suddenly caught Nathaniel by surprise and with it came a flood of thoughts and feelings. He began to feel tears well up in his eyes, and that was a feeling he certainly was not comfortable with. "I… I'm sorry, Moses," Nathaniel stammered as he turned and began walking away.

"Wait a minute, Nathaniel. Come back here!" Moses pleaded.

But there was no way that Nathaniel could, for at that moment he felt a tear run down his cheek, which ignited a full color of red in his face. He could never let anyone see him like that, especially Moses. He broke into a slow run and was gone.

The vote was only nine days away. Spring was waging its yearly battle with winter as it slowly melted winter's icy hand off the land. Construction work was picking up and Nathaniel worked long hours that week. It seemed all he did was come home to sleep, wake up, and then go to work again. Construction was hard physical work, exhausting work, and it took time for his body to make the adjustment. He had no time for his regular discussions with Reverend McDermit, or with anybody else for that matter. Nathaniel was distraught about that, but he really had no choice. Moreover, Nathaniel was still feeling awkward and embarrassed about their last encounter, and it seemed to him that Reverend McDermit didn't want to talk about the church situation anyway. He felt at a loss about what he should or shouldn't say in front of Moses anymore, and thought that he would probably just end up annoying his friend more than comforting him. Besides, the job Nathaniel was working on was only temporary, and he would have more time the following week to stop over and visit with Reverend McDermit.

By 6:45 p.m. on Saturday, April 1, the pews of Mount Calvary Church were already filled and the ushers were frantically pulling out the folding chairs. Nathaniel had put in a long day, not getting home until after 6 p.m. He went home, cleaned up, and rushed over to the church, arriving at 7:05 p.m. There was not a seat left, only standing room in the very back.

Moses was nowhere to be seen. Charlie Fitch sat in the front row, surrounded by Bud Masters and two of the men who had attended his late night "Bible study." They all sat there, looking self-important and dignified, knowing—or perhaps thinking—that everyone in the church had one eye on them. Charlie had a look on his face that can only be described as the proverbial "cat that ate the canary." This was his day; he had worked hard for it and he was going to enjoy it.

Marvin Olafson soon made his way onto the empty platform and then to the microphone at the pulpit.

"This meeting of Mount Calvary Church is now in progress. The congregation will refrain at this point from any conversation or disturbances. This meeting was called by the church board in response to concerns over the future leadership of our church. Right now, before I go on, I want to make something perfectly clear," he said sternly. "There has never been any question as to the mental competency, uprightness, or integrity of our current pastor, Reverend Moses McDermit. That is not why we're here tonight. Anyone who has suggested otherwise has been spreading false gossip and should be ashamed of themselves," he admonished, appearing to take a quick glance over at Bud Masters and his cohorts.

"I'm not going to drag this out. We will not hear any testimony one way or the other. Let me remind you that you may only vote if you are a regular member of Mount Calvary Church. You will be handed a piece of paper and a pencil; when you are instructed, simply write 'yes' on it if you feel that Reverend Moses McDermit should remain as pastor. Write 'no' if you do not." He then repeated the instructions. "When you are done, fold your ballots and pass them to the left, where an usher will collect them. The votes will then be tallied and I will announce the results."

Marvin Olafson led a short prayer for guidance. The ballots were then handed out, and within a half-hour they were collected and counted. Marvin again made his way to the microphone.

"The votes have been tallied, and the results are fifty-three votes for Reverend Moses McDermit to remain as pastor of Mount Calvary Church and two hundred sixty-one opposed. According to the organizational rules adopted by this church, assistant pastor Charlie Fitch will now assume the role of interim pastor of Mount Calvary Church until such time as another vote will be taken regarding qualified candidates aspiring to assume the role of pastor here."

Charlie Fitch tried very hard to appear refined and humble, but it just wasn't in him. He couldn't stop the smug grin that kept creeping across his face.

Then, seemingly out of nowhere, Reverend Moses McDermit could be seen making his way across the platform toward the microphone. Marvin Olafson saw him out of the corner of his eye and discreetly departed. The elderly minister slowly walked across the platform, cane in hand providing support. The church became as quiet as a tomb as all eyes followed him. The creaking of the wood beneath his feet and the plop of his cane as he set it down with each step seemed to be magnified as he made his way. It seemed to take an eternity for him to reach that microphone. Charlie Fitch began shifting nervously in his seat.

Finally reaching the pulpit, Moses propped his cane against it, grasped the lectern firmly with both hands and stood there for a moment. He closed his eyes and patted the pulpit gently, like it was an old friend. He looked very old and tired now; every wrinkle and every line on his face seemed deeper and more pronounced than they had been just days before, and it appeared as if he were carrying the weight of the world on his shoulders

"My friends," he softly began "today, you have chosen a new direction, a new road to travel down. I hope and pray that it is a successful one," he said quietly and calmly, pausing for a moment as he gathered his thoughts. "You know, I can hardly believe it was fifty years ago that I came to you. So much has changed in the world, in this church. I was a young man when I arrived, strong-willed, and maybe a little bull-headed," he acknowledged with a reserved smile. "Some of the decisions I have had to make as your pastor weren't very popular. I'm sure that sometimes some people thought I was just being downright mean. Those times, when I felt led by God to take those stands, were some of the loneliest periods of my life. If I could have, I would have loved to take an easier road, compromised in some of the situations," he confessed. "But please believe me when I tell you that everything I did, I did with your best interests at heart," he said as he reached into the top pocket of his suit coat and pulled out a handkerchief. He brought it to his face and dabbed at his eyes.

"You know, I think that the worst feeling in the world must be when you love someone or something with all your heart, and then one day it hits you between the eyes that the affection is not being returned. Rejection is perhaps one of life's cruelest blows, for there is very little that one can say or do to remedy another's feeling of indifference." He stopped, and then, as an afterthought, added "I suppose that God must feel that way quite often."

Some women in the congregation were now also bringing handkerchiefs to their eyes. The cockiness that Charlie Fitch, Bud Masters, and the other men had been displaying disintegrated into a combination of unease and conviction.

"I guess... this is my last sermon to you, if that is what this is. I want you to know that I have loved you as a father loves his children. I leave you today a little broken-hearted, but not embittered. I ask for your forgiveness if I have offended any one of you, and I also ask that you keep me in your prayers. May God bless you all. Goodbye, my friends."

Reverend Moses McDermit began to turn and reach for his cane, but unexpectedly turned back and grabbed the top of the pulpit with both hands. He suddenly gasped, shut his eyes tightly, and hunched over forward. He bent over and rested his white head and shoulders on the lectern, his strong hands still holding on to the pulpit, his knuckles white from the grip he had on it.

For a moment that seemed to last an eternity, nobody did anything, perhaps not wanting to believe what was happening in front of them. Then a woman shrieked, and another screamed, "Help him! Dear God, somebody help him!"

Finally, Marvin Olafson was beside Moses, with his arm around him, unsuccessfully trying to pull him away and lay him down. He soon realized that Moses' hands were so tightly clenched to the pulpit that he had to pull them off. Nathaniel, who had been at the very back of the church, pushed and shoved his way through the alarmed congregation. Charlie Fitch stood pale and still, as though in a trance.

Someone ran for a phone and dialed 911, while Marvin and Nathaniel feverishly performed CPR. It all began to have a rather surreal feeling about it—nightmarish, as though everything was happening in slow motion. Nobody could seem to move quite fast enough or think clearly enough. Something like this couldn't be happening; not in this fine church.

Nathaniel rode with Moses and a paramedic in the back of the ambulance as it screamed toward the hospital. Moses' eyes were closed, his skin a sickly gray. Every line in his face seemed to have deepened, and he looked much older than he had appeared less than an hour before. His breathing was heavy and labored, as if his body was willing itself to remain alive. Nathaniel held the old man's cold hand tightly, muttering prayers and assuring Moses that he was going to be all right. Suddenly he noticed Moses' face wince and his eyes begin to flutter.

"Where… what happened… where am I?" he whispered in a gravelly voice.

"Reverend McDermit, it's me, Nathaniel. We're in an ambulance, we're on our way to the hospital. You fainted at the church. You're going to be OK… just relax."

Moses' eyes were cloudy and only half open as he slowly looked over at the young paramedic who was monitoring his vital signs. The man smiled and nodded. The paramedic explained that they weren't completely sure what had happened yet but that Moses may have had a heart attack. He told Moses to just try to stay calm and comfortable until they got to the hospital. Moses' eyes then slowly made their way back to Nathaniel. He remained still for a few moments and then closed his eyes. When he opened them again the cloudiness seemed to have left, and while he still looked frail and gray, a certain strength seemed to shine from within him. "This is my time," he whispered to Nathaniel. There almost seemed to be a hint of joy in his voice.

"Your time?" Nathaniel asked, not sure if he had heard him correctly.

"There is a season for everything..." said Moses.

The paramedic interrupted. "Sir, you really shouldn't talk right now." Moses looked the young man square in the eye, poker-faced, and said nothing. "Uh... well... you shouldn't be exerting yourself." Moses, even while dying, was still the leader. The man looked a little embarrassed and self-conscious and turned to observe a monitor.

"I am going, Nathaniel. I feel him calling me and I know his voice. My reward is near and I want to go. I need to go. Son, don't let bitterness rob you of the wonderful things God has for you. And he does have wonderful things!" Oddly, Moses almost seemed to be gaining his strength back; his voice was stronger, and Nathaniel felt his hand being gripped tightly.

"Remember, don't look at what men do—look at what God can do with them despite their faults and flaws. That's the miracle, Nathaniel! Pray for those who might despitefully use you. There is no gain in hating them. God must increase and you must become less." Moses' face almost seemed to be shining now. The paramedic couldn't help notice what was occurring and gazed on in stunned silence.

Moses then almost shouted, "For, Nathaniel... greater is he that is in you, than he that is in the world!" Moses had both his hands wrapped tightly over Nathaniel's. There was a joy mixed with excitement in his eyes.

But just as quickly as Moses seemed to gain his strength back, he was gone. Nathaniel, whose gaze was fixed into Moses' eyes could see the light fade and dim in them. The hands that had felt so strong began to loosen their grip. A deep peace seemed to come over Moses' face. He had a hint of a smile on his lips as his eyes closed for the last time.

"Pastor, no! You are still needed!" Nathaniel cried, tears streaming down his face as he knelt beside his pastor. But the fact was that Moses was gone. And even Moses, the man with the iron resolve, could not will himself back to life.

"Hypocrites." Nathaniel mumbled under his breath as he noted the bouquets of flowers lining the walls of the funeral parlor. "This man gave you the best years of his life and after destroying him, you think that a bouquet of flowers makes up for it. I hope the flowers sooth your consciences, if you have any left," he declared, sarcasm dripping from his voice.

"You didn't know Reverend McDermit very well if you think that this destroyed him. Take my word for it; it didn't destroy him. So don't let it destroy you."

Nathaniel jumped—he had thought he was alone. Two figures stood in the shadows in the back of the room near the doorway.

"Who are you, and how long have you been standing there?" Nathaniel growled.

"Oh, we've been standing here long enough," one of them answered as they stepped from the shadows.

They were two old men. One was short, slightly overweight, and balding. The other, tall, with a full head of distinguished-looking gray hair. "My name is Ron Desmond, and this is Andrew Sutain," he said extending his hand, "and I would guess that you might be Nathaniel O'Brien."

Nathaniel's face began to light up, "Yes, yes, I remember Reverend McDermit mentioning your names! You are friends of his from way back, aren't you?"

"Yes, way, way back!" Andrew Sutain responded, grinning.

"About five or six years ago, shortly after Reverend Fitch came here, the two of us, along with our wives, decided we had had altogether enough of these Minnesota winters and retired to Phoenix, Arizona," Ron began. "I can see nothing has changed, for here it is April and you still have to lug around a winter coat! I don't miss that, no sir! You people really ought to do something about your winters!" Andrew laughed and nodded his head in agreement.

"Well, we've kept in contact with Reverend McDermit; we'd get a phone call or send a letter. You see, the Reverend was like family to us."

"Yes, like family," Andrew chimed in.

"He called us just last week and said he needed our prayers. He didn't go into specifics, but it was pretty easy to figure out what was going on here. We still have friends and relatives who live here. I cried like a baby when I got the phone call Sunday morning and they told me what had happened," Ron explained as he pulled a tissue from a box on a nearby stand and blew his nose.

"You know, when Reverend Fitch came here and we had that vote, there was something about him, something familiar, that Andrew and I just weren't comfortable with."

"No, we weren't," Andrew added.

"It was strange. I mean, the way he and his wife could sing and preach, how could anything be wrong? But we just couldn't shake that feeling. In fact Andrew and I were the only ones who voted against him; even our wives wouldn't go along with us. I tried to bring it up to Moses once shortly after that, but he would hear none of it—he was real protective of the ministry, you know."

"Yeah, I know," Nathaniel answered somberly.

"Well, we had kind of forgotten about it, and it wasn't until Andrew and I were back in Lexington that we figured out what it was. All of a sudden, it was déjà vu! That feeling, only stronger now, something very familiar about it. So real we could just about touch it." Ron seemed almost lost to himself as he held his hands in front of him, opening and closing them as if he were grabbing for something.

"All of a sudden Andrew looked at me and said, 'Reverend Fitch.

That spirit about him… something so familiar. That feeling we used to have when we had trouble in the church all those years back. There's something about him. His presence reminds me of your brother.' And I knew that instant what he meant! Mind you, they looked nothing alike! But you see, before Reverend McDermit first came here, the two of us here and my brother Don, who, you might say, was the ringleader, caused this church a whole lot of trouble. Oh, we were convinced that what we were doing was right, I'd say clear to the bone, especially my brother. But when Reverend McDermit arrived and rebuked us, it was almost as if we awoke from a dream. We all eventually repented and suddenly it became very clear, like a fog had lifted, that what we had been doing was wrong. That first night when Reverend Fitch was up there preaching, we felt that strange spirit again—like a chilly breeze coming down the back of your neck. It was very, very weak, but something about him left Andrew and me feeling uncomfortable. There wasn't anything that he said or did that we could put our finger on, and it wasn't until we just arrived back here that we put it all together. It was that same spirit from the old days that had troubled our church! We recognized it. Only it feels even stronger here now."

Nathaniel was only slightly interested in their story. It was nice to meet some old friends of Moses, but Nathaniel had had his fill of Christians and Christianity. Hearing these two old men speculate on Reverend Fitch and their theory about him only strengthened Nathaniel's growing suspicion that much of Christianity was built on superstition and hucksterism. It was becoming clear to him now that much of it preyed on the simple-minded and the easily led, and Reverend Charlie Fitch was someone who was either smart enough or corrupt enough to realize that. What was that old saying, Nathaniel thought, "Fool me once, shame on you; fool me twice shame on me." No, he certainly wasn't going to be fooled again.

"Listen, thank you for sharing that with me. It's been good to meet some old friends of Reverend McDermit," Nathaniel said and glanced down at his watch. "Will you look at the time? It's almost seven o' clock, so I really need to get going. Again, it was nice meeting both of you," he stated as he held out his hand.

"It didn't destroy him, you know, if that's what you think," Ron Desmond countered as he shook Nathaniel's hand.

"What...?" questioned Nathaniel

"I heard what you were saying when we walked in. Sure, it was a terrible thing that happened, what they did to him. But I know Reverend Moses McDermit. It was the people that he was worried about, what was going to happen to them. He wasn't concerned about himself. He cared for them like they were his own flesh and blood, and I'm sure if you could ask him right now he'd tell you he still feels the same way about them. His faith and spirit weren't destroyed and that's what's important. The reason I knew who you were right away was because Moses told me about you, about what high hopes he had for you. He spoke about you like you were his son. Don't become bitter over what happened. If you really were a friend of Reverend McDermit, that's the last thing he would want you to do."

But Nathaniel would have none of it, his mind was made up. "Thank you, both of you, for your concern. I can tell you were very good friends of his, but I really must be going now," Nathaniel hurried over to the coatrack, quickly pushed his arms through the sleeves of his coat, and made his way to the front door, and stepped outside.

Nathaniel stood on the sidewalk in front of the funeral home and took a deep breath of cold spring air. It was dusk and he stared blindly at the headlights of the cars as they played back and forth in front of him on the busy city street, trying to block out anything the old men had told him that might have made sense.

"At least it's spring," he told himself, and started toward his car. He was about to round the corner of the building when he reached into his pants pocket and pulled out his car keys. There, with his other keys, was that old skeleton key Moses had given him.

"Greater is he that is in you, than he that is in the world. 1st John 4:4," Nathaniel said out loud. He suddenly felt a pang of remorse and looked up at the stars that were beginning to come out. "Dear God, if you're really out there, help me. None of this makes sense to me anymore. Please, God, please…" Nathaniel stopped his prayer, for he heard a group of people talking around the corner.

"God bless you, sister, your prayers are most certainly welcome right now, I'll need them more than ever." Nathaniel recognized the voice of Charlie Fitch.

"This has to be very hard on you, Reverend, and you, too, Mrs. Fitch. It's too bad this had to happen, right when you are taking over the ministry. Reverend McDermit should have stepped down years ago. Why he had to cause the church so much pain and suffering I'll never know! He was a stubborn man; everyone knew that. Oh, I'll not speak ill of the dead. In his time he was a fine man, but he just stayed too long, bless his heart. I know how hard you tried to explain to him about how this church needed that new program of yours; everybody knows that. It's no secret that he was suffering from hardening of the arteries, and you know what that does to the mind, the poor soul," the woman said as she grabbed Charlie's hand and patted it.

"Well, I honestly did try; but as you said, Reverend McDermit was rather set in his ways. I remember a time last fall when I went over my program with him, and I wondered at the time whether he really understood it. If that's true what you say about his hardening of the arteries, that would explain a lot of things. We may never know the full weight that Reverend McDermit carried in his last years of life, God bless him. It is truly sad the way things turned out, but the church will rebound, for as the good book says, all things work towards the good for those who love the Lord."

"God bless you, Pastor, for your strength and wisdom in this difficult time," another voice said.

"I've done very little, my friends. Look, we better quit our gabbing and pay our last respects to Reverend McDermit."

Nathaniel heard the footsteps coming toward the corner. He took a few steps backward and leaned up against the front of the brick building.

A group of seven people came around the corner, led by the tall, polished reverend and his beautiful wife. They would have walked right past Nathaniel, not even noticing him, if he hadn't spoken up, "Well, isn't this a sight. The loyal assistant pastor and the heartbroken congregation paying their last respects to their beloved pastor. Excuse me if I start crying. Charlie, feel free to use my handkerchief if emotion overwhelms you."

The startled group all did a little hop at the first sound of Nathaniel's voice, and his words hit them like a bucket of icy water as they turned to see where it came from. "Who... who is that, who said that?" someone in the group called out. They all peered toward the voice and the figure that stood against the wall in the shadow of the overhanging eve. Nathaniel stepped forward.

"I'm sorry to interrupt, really I am. You see I couldn't help but overhear all those wonderful things you all had to say. What a wonderful and remarkable bunch of human beings you all are."

Jennifer Fitch huddled closer to Charlie. "Who is that?" she nervously asked her husband.

Charlie Fitch took a few steps toward Nathaniel, "Oh, it's you, Daniel. It's Daniel, honey, that guy who was always hanging around and bothering Reverend McDermit. What's the problem, Daniel?"

"Oh-h-h-h, I don't know, I seem to have so many problems these days. When I think about it, a lot of them are coming from you and your group of upstanding church members right here, bless your souls. Come to think of it, you're probably the biggest bunch of deceitful, untrustworthy, backstabbing, arrogant chameleons I have ever met. Bless your black little hearts!"

Charlie turned toward his wife. "You and the other women better go inside. I'll take care of this."

Jennifer and three other horrified women quickly scurried in through the front door of the mortuary.

"Oh, I'm sorry, Charlie. Did I offend them? I guess I haven't learned to tear someone apart as neatly and politely as you folks yet."

"I think you better leave before you get yourself in trouble, boy. Go ahead, get out of here! Imagine that, causing trouble at Reverend McDermit's wake. What a prize you are! Now get out of here before

I call the police," Charlie threatened, the two other men standing by his side.

"I'll leave all right, but only when I'm through. You might fool these people, Fitch, but you're not fooling me. I just heard you tell that woman about how you tried to explain to Reverend McDermit about your grand plans. How you told her that he didn't understand it and then both of you making innuendoes about Reverend McDermit being senile. Well guess what, 'friend'—I was doing some painting underneath that open window on that warm afternoon, some touch-up work on his siding, and I heard the whole thing. Tell the truth now—Reverend McDermit wasn't confused about anything that day, was he? C'mon, Fitch. Clue everyone in on what your beloved pastor was confused about. I was there, Fitch. I heard it all!"

Charlie Fitch's face began to boil with anger; his eyes seemed to want to pop from his head. "Why you sneaky… You seem to be pretty good at eavesdropping aren't you, son? I'm not going to stand here and listen to these lies one more minute!" he yelled, taking a long-legged stride toward Nathaniel. The two other men, not sure what to do, stayed where they were.

Charlie came up on Nathaniel's right side and grabbed him by the back of his neck. He was a good six inches taller and easily fifty pounds heavier than Nathaniel. It appeared to be quite a mismatch, and it was. "Now get out of here before I have you thrown in jail!" he screamed in Nathaniel's ear, squeezing his neck and pushing him forward toward the parking lot.

"I'm going to say this just one time. Let go of my neck or you will lose the use of your arm, Fitch," Nathaniel replied calmly but intensely."

"You leave this place now!" Charlie screamed again in his ear, squeezing Nathaniel's neck harder.

The next sound that everyone heard was a loud "Ooaaaf!" coming from Charlie Fitch as Nathaniel's elbow went crashing into Charlie's soft stomach. Both of Charlie's hands immediately flew up in the air from the jolt. Nathaniel quickly turned toward Charlie, grabbed his left wrist with his right hand, and placed his left hand under Charlie's left biceps. He then pushed slightly backward on Charlie's wrist.

"AAAAGHHHHHH! Please don't, please don't break my arm!" Charlie begged, as he dropped to his knees, screaming in pain. Nathaniel cast a menacing glance at the other two men; it was obvious they wanted no part of this.

"Well, what have you got to say for yourself now, Mr. Fitch? Not too much, it sounds like. Can you imagine that? This has got to be a first, Charlie. You usually have so much to say! What was that, Charlie, I didn't quite get that? I suppose that…"

"Let go of him! What in the world do you think you're doing! What would Reverend McDermit say if he could see you now?" It was Ron Desmond, and standing beside him was Andrew Sutain. Nathaniel let go of Charlie's arm. Fitch dropped to the ground in a heap, evidently having fainted.

"You see he attacked me… grabbed my neck… you saw what he did," he said pointing to the two other men. Jennifer Fitch suddenly came screaming out the front door.

"What have you done to my husband? You animal! Someone call the police!" she screamed as she ran over to Charlie, who was beginning to mutter nonsense as he was coming to.

Nathaniel turned and ran as fast as he could, away from the screaming, the accusations, and the commotion. He jumped into his truck, started the engine, and slammed the gas pedal to the floor. The tires squealed, and he was gone.

CHAPTER SEVEN

Mountains to Climb

Nathaniel roared down the city streets, causing the puddles and rivers of melting snow in the road to explode as he drove through them. He made his way to the freeway, where he caught Highway 61 north. All he wanted to do now was go home. He wondered if anyone at the mortuary had called the police, and if at any moment he might be seeing the flashing red lights of a police car in his rearview mirror. Adrenaline was pumping through him, and his hands shook on the steering wheel.

"This is what I get for praying!" he shouted out loud.

He was convinced now more than ever that his religious experience had been a farce and that whatever religious encounter he had supposedly experienced had more to do with emotion than reality. If God was in control, why had he let all of this happen? And what about all those people at Mount Calvary who claimed to represent God, claimed to be Christians? He had met more compassionate people at work or in bars. But had the whole thing really been a farce? What about Reverend McDermit and others he had met who did display what one would consider the attributes of Christ? Could that be disregarded? Nathaniel's mind went back and forth as his thoughts and emotions did battle with one another.

"Agnosticism looks pretty good right now," he said aloud. "Maybe that's it," he thought. "Maybe man was never meant to understand or have close contact with God… that would explain a lot of things. I'm reaching out to something that cannot or should not be touched. I'm trying to do something that shouldn't be done. Can't be done. All this has been a sign, and I've been just too stupid to understand it. That's it. That's it!" He repeated the thought over in his mind a few times, trying to convince himself of its merits. But he felt a voice deep inside tell him, "That's not it."

He left the highway and traveled east on Beam Avenue. He was almost home now, just another couple miles. Suddenly, the motor of his truck died, with no coughing or spitting—no warning at all. Nathaniel turned the key back and forth in the ignition, but the only sound was the jingling of his keys.

"Oh, great, this tops off a perfect evening!" Nathaniel shouted in anger at the top of his lungs. He pulled the truck over to the side of the road as it coasted to a stop. He again began wiggling his key back and forth, with no success. He yanked the keys from the ignition and crammed them into his pocket. It was dark and he had no flashlight or tools, so he was helpless. He sat there motionless, the rage building in him about the truck, the wake, Reverend McDermit, his life. Suddenly he exploded, his right fist crashing into the windshield and then into the dashboard, leaving cracks in both. He stepped out of the truck, blood dripping from his knuckles, and slammed the door as hard as he could.

It was a fairly deserted street, with a golf course to the north on the other side of the street. To the south was a dirt driveway that led to the city composting site that was surrounded by woods. The apartment where Nathaniel lived was on the other side of those woods. If he went east and stayed on Beam and the paved streets, he would have to double back to reach his home, adding almost another mile to his walk. Nathaniel didn't feel like walking; he just wanted to go home and let sleep give him an escape from his inner conflicts. He decided to take the shortcut through the woods and headed down the entrance road toward the composting site.

He zipped his light jacket as high as it would go; at night it could still dip below freezing, and tonight was one of those nights. It was a long, dark, and lonely looking dirt driveway that continued for a quarter of a mile. Nathaniel could hear the sounds of the cars on Highway 61 about a half-mile away. It was the only distraction from the crunching of his footsteps as he walked the dirt and gravel road.

He reached the composting site, and through the darkness he could see the great mounds of leaves and composted soil, some of them reaching sixty feet high or taller, looking like miniature mountains. It had a strange look to it at night, and he could almost imagine he was on another planet.

Nathaniel was still very much full of adrenaline and decided to try to wear some of it off. He ran up the first pile of compost, reached the top, and jumped. He landed on the side of the hill just a few yards below, and his momentum sent him tumbling head over heels to the bottom. He lay on the cold ground for a while, laughing at himself, and laughing just because it felt so good. He eventually got to his feet and ran up and down the next pile, and then the next, and then the next one after that. He ran up one more and collapsed at the top, his lungs inhaling the cold air as fast as they could and his legs feeling like they were made of rubber. He remembered that he had once read about a football player, a great running back, who stayed in shape in the off-season by running up and down sand dunes. It was very clear to Nathaniel now why he did it, for it was a tremendous workout.

He sat up, still breathing heavily. He was physically tired but feeling much better emotionally. The exercise had helped clear his head and he was feeling more like his old self. Nathaniel slowly got to his feet and made his way down the mound to the level ground. He was in the middle of the composting site now. The farther he walked into the area, the more the older piles were decomposing, and beginning to look like dirt. He knew that he had to be nearing the woods now. In another ten minutes he would be home. It was funny, he thought, how quiet it was out here, how the mounds of compost must insulate the sound because he could no longer hear the highway. Or anything at all for that matter, save his own breathing and footsteps.

He walked another ten minutes but still did not reach the woods. He decided to climb a nearby pile and see if he could figure out where he was. It was very dark now, and he could not make out much of anything unless he was very close to it.

When he reached the top, he could see nothing familiar. In fact, Nathaniel could see nothing but the outline of the mounds closest to him. He looked up into the sky and did a double take. He had never seen so many stars in his life. The sky was exploding with them. He knew that getting away from the city lights gave one a better view of the stars, but he couldn't recall ever seeing this many before. After all, he didn't live too terribly far from here. Oh, well, he thought,   he could figure this out later, because right now he just wanted to go home.

"I must have veered off and got turned around," he said out loud. He wasn't quite sure how to get his bearing back.

"Wait a minute, now that I'm on top of a mound, I should be able to hear the cars on Highway 61, west of here. That will give me some direction," he remarked as he paused and listened. He heard nothing. Absolutely nothing.

"That's strange; even on a Wednesday night you would think you would hear a few cars. It can't be that late." He had no watch on him, but he estimated it could be no later than 9 p.m. He was starting to feel warm, so he loosened his jacket. "It's amazing what a little exercise will do. My hands aren't even cold," he thought, opening and closing them.

"What to do? What to do?" he said out loud. He was beginning to feel rather stupid about the whole thing.

He decided to head in the same direction he had been going, following as straight a path as possible. He scrambled down, but even the ground felt different now. It was softer than before and filled his shoes. He finally sat down and emptied out a shoe. What poured out through his fingers felt odd. Instead of lumpy compost dirt, it felt very fine. Almost like sand.

"I wonder what they've been dumping back here? This sure does-n't feel like compost or dirt," he thought. He put his shoes back on and started walking again. His shoes promptly filled again, but he decided to ignore it and kept on walking.

Fifteen minutes later he was still walking. Now Nathaniel was total-ly confused, for no matter which direction he'd chosen, he should have reached the end by now. The composting area simply was not that big. He was feeling even warmer now, so he took off his jacket, tied the arms around his waist, and sat down on the side of a mound. His hands sank into the side of the hill; he clenched a fistful of soil and brought it close to his face.

"This is not compost, this is sand!" he shouted as it ran through his fingers. He studied the piles around him, and even in the darkness he could tell these were now lighter in color than the first compost hills he had come across. "These all look like sand!" he shouted.

Nathaniel ran to the top of the mound he had been sitting beside to see if he could get a better view, but it was just too dark. He dropped to his knees, pounding his fists into the mound with frustration. He felt not only confused, but also a total fool. How in the world could he have managed to get lost in a composting area that couldn't be much larger than half of a square mile! He was also starting to get very thirsty as his body demanded replenishment from all of that evening's excite-ment and exercise.

Nathaniel lay down on his back, staring up at the stars again, his mind going in circles. Why hadn't he just taken the paved roads? He'd have been home right now. It had been stupid to have tried a shortcut in the dark. All the negative feelings from the last few days were return-ing, along with his bubbling anger at himself and others. He let out a bellow as the rage and frustration suddenly consumed him. He jumped to his feet and started running as fast and as hard as he could, not caring where he ran. He felt like a trapped animal and he wanted out. He would find his way out of this place and he wouldn't stop running until he did.

It wasn't long before his legs began to feel like rubber again. Running in sand, as he had found out earlier, takes its toll quickly. But he pressed on, his anger and frustration fueling him. Nathaniel was a determined fellow by nature, even more so when he was aggravated. And he was feeling very aggravated at the moment. He ignored his thirst and his burning legs and kept running.

"Left foot, right foot, left foot, right foot," was all he was concentrating on now as his legs began to grow numb with fatigue. The mounds seemed to be leveling off now; that was good. "Now I'm getting somewhere," he thought.

"Left foot, right foot, left foot, right foot." He was gasping for air, but he continued, disregarding all the signals his body was sending him. Nathaniel was becoming utterly exhausted, but as the mounds began to subside, he suddenly felt a ray of hope and it drove him on. He gritted his teeth and thought, "I'm almost out of here, just a little farther and I'm out of here."

Suddenly his legs began to wobble and then went out from under him, sending him diving forward. His hands went forward to cushion his fall but it was too late. He landed on the ground face first, filling his open mouth with sand. He tried to spit it out, but his mouth was so dry the sand stuck to the insides. He shook his head violently back and forth, like a terrier shaking a rat. He began coughing and gasping for breath, clawing at his mouth, trying to clean it out with his fingers. He was breathing so hard and so heavily that he was afraid he might inhale some of the sand into his lungs.

He rolled around for some time in complete misery and madness, clutching at his mouth as it screamed to him for water. It seemed an eternity, but his breathing finally slowed enough for him to regain some measure of lucidity.

Nathaniel rolled onto his side and began to spit, trying to clear his mouth of as much sand as possible. His lips were burning now also from dryness and from the impact of having fallen face first.

"Where am I? Where in the world am I?" he desperately wondered. His breathing was returning to normal and he had spit and dug out most of the sand from his mouth. His face and neck were caked with sand, the sweat having provided a good adhesive for it when he fell. He looked and felt miserable.

He was out of ideas and his nosedive into the sand had tempered his anger and energy. For the moment, the only thing he could think of was to lie there and recuperate. He began brushing the sand off his face and slapping at the side of his head to remove the sand in his ear and hair.

Suddenly he heard a noise. It sounded almost like the wind when it makes its way through the trees; a rushing sound. Was it noise from the cars on Highway 61? No, wait, that wasn't it either, this was different. What was it? It sounded like—no that was impossible, there wasn't any around here—wait... yes! There it was again! The sounds of waves of water rushing in to meet the shore. But how could that be? He had lived here long enough to know there were no lakes near the composting area. Silver Lake was the nearest lake that came to mind, and that was three or four miles northeast of where he had started. He would have had to have crossed busy roads to get there.

He lay still and listened again. Yes, that had to be water. Nathaniel tried to do some figuring in his head, but none of it made sense. He got up slowly and stood on shaky legs. The mounds were all but gone now, though the ground was still sand. He was terribly thirsty, and the sound of water called to him. He wanted to run, but his body objected. Step by step the sound grew louder and louder.

Suddenly, through the blackness, he saw it. It was a tremendous body of water! He had no idea at the moment how or why it was there. He didn't care. All that mattered was that it was water. He wanted it, and it was within walking distance! The sight seemed to revive him, so he picked up his pace.

"Just thirty feet more, just twenty-five feet more," he began to count down as he neared the water. His thirst seemed to grow with each step, anticipating the relief it would give to him. Suddenly he was there, crawling down the last few feet of the beach on his hands and knees. The cool water came over his legs and up to his elbows, soaking his pants and shirt, and he let out a whoop for joy. He plunged his head deep into the water and felt the sand and sweat leave his face. He began to drink long, almost loving, deep drinks of the cool water.

But something was wrong. His eyes began to burn and a horrible salty taste began to fill his mouth. His thirst had been so strong that at first he ignored it, but it grew and grew until his head shot out of the water. Eyes bulging wide, he let out a horrible gurgling scream. He rose to his feet, vomiting and coughing. He stumbled backward onto the beach and landed on his back, his head coming down upon something hard. The stars in the sky began to spin and then all was black.

CHAPTER EIGHT

Ethan

•

Oh, there's coming a time when we'll all be free,
Look up Michael, we're almost home,
So get the table ready, set a place for me
Look up Gabriel, we're almost home.

Six thousand, six thousand years!
Look up Michael, we're almost home,
Seen a whole lot of trouble, a whole lot of tears,
Look up Gabriel, we're almost home.

Slowly regaining his senses, Nathaniel was somewhere between the conscious and unconscious. He was dreaming—a waiter with a deep-voiced baritone sang this song as he served Nathaniel in an open-air restaurant. Nathaniel sat in a comfortable wicker chair, sunning himself as the waiter served him glass after glass of cold ice water. He drank and drank and then drank some more, with the waiter singing and faithfully refilling his cup. But no matter how many times it was refilled, the water just wouldn't quench his thirst.

Nathaniel's eyes fluttered and daylight peeked in between his lids. His mind went back and forth between the restaurant and the daylight, not sure which one it wanted. Nathaniel swallowed, and the pain and unpleasantness of that action pushed his mind closer into reality. "I'm so thirsty, so terribly thirsty," he moaned to himself. He thought he caught the smell of something cooking. It smelled good, like fish frying on a grill.

"It must be from the restaurant," he mumbled and began to doze again. "Wait a minute," he thought as his mind began to clear. "I'm not at a restaurant. Where am I?"

He was lying flat on his back, and when he forced one eye open Nathaniel saw a beautiful blue sky. It soon occurred to him, as the fog lifted from his mind and he became fully cognizant, that the singing from his dream had not stopped! He turned his head slowly to the left, and through squinting eyes saw the back of a very large man squatting next to a fire. He closed his eyes and quickly tried to gather his thoughts. The rancid taste in his mouth and his horrible thirst pleaded with him for attention, but he pushed them aside. Where was he? Oh, yes, now it was coming back to him. The wake, the fight, lost in the composting hills, the water. Oh, that terrible water! But again, where was he and who was this man?

He opened his eyes again and took a second look at the back of the stranger. He was oddly dressed, to say the least. It appeared that he was wearing a long white flowing cloak or robe, with a large hood that hung down in the back. His hair, coal black and wavy, ended at the back of his collar. Apart from his strange clothes, the thing that was most impressive about him was his build. His shoulders appeared as if they were twice as wide as Nathaniel's. His left arm, which hung by his side, was somewhat hidden by a flowing sleeve. But his wrist, which Nathaniel could see, was the size of a two-by-four, and his hand the size of a small ham.

Nathaniel lay there trying to come up with some explanation for this fellow. He knew that there was some type of monastery just east of Oakdale. It had always seemed very secretive and mysterious to him. In his youth, Nathaniel and his friends used to drive by it to try to catch a glimpse of the people who lived there. Maybe this man was some kind of deformed monk who had wandered away from the grounds.

The man continued to sing and tend to his fire, seemingly oblivious to Nathaniel, who remained motionless, moving nothing but his eyes, not sure what to do. It crossed his mind that if this man wasn't a deformed monk, he could be someone even stranger. He had no desire to scuffle with a madman roughly the size of a mini-van. Nathaniel was less than five yards from the robed figure, and he decided the first thing he should do is put some more space between them. He was starting to quietly roll backwards when the man reached around his neck and pulled a strap up over his head. He grabbed whatever was attached to the strap and tossed it on the ground between them. The sound of liquid echoing inside a metal container immediately caught Nathaniel's attention. His eyes quickly discovered that it was a canteen, and judging by the sound, it was heavy with water.

This suddenly changed everything. He was almost delirious with thirst, and the sound of the liquid in the canteen tormented him even the more. He began to tremble with desire. Whether the canteen's owner was a madman or a deformed monk, Nathaniel had to have some of that water, or whatever it was, one way or another. Finally, his wariness gave way to his desire. "Excuse me," he began to say, but nothing but an inaudible whisper came out. He tried to swallow and clear his throat, but there was no moisture in his throat to assist him. "Excuse me," he tried again, attempting to increase his volume, which only produced a rather comical sounding, high squeaky voice. "May I have a drink from your canteen?"

The robed figure stopped his singing, but didn't turn around. He poked at the fire a few times with a stick. Then he spoke, "It seems a little ill-mannered to ask a total stranger to drink from his canteen, doesn't it?"

"I'm sorry," Nathaniel rasped. "You see, I can hardly talk. Last night…"

"Go ahead," The man interjected, though still with his back to him.

"You mean I can have a drink?" he asked cautiously.

"Drink all you want."

Nathaniel slowly rose to his feet and approached the man and his canteen. His wariness returned as he came closer. What was in the canteen, and what if it was drugged? Maybe this man was part of some satanic cult that had had this whole thing planned out. Maybe, some-how, they had drugged him last night. That would explain a lot of things. And why would this man decide to build a fire and make him-self comfortable just a few feet from an unconscious stranger? Nathaniel now stood just a few feet behind him. He hesitated momen-tarily, but his overpowering thirst forced him to bend down and pick up the canteen.

Nathaniel kept one eye on the back of the man as he unscrewed the top. He sniffed at the opening of the canteen. It was water, and he had never smelled anything sweeter in his life. He thrust the opening of the canteen past his cracked lips and into his mouth, and began drinking in great sloppy gulps. He thought that perhaps he shouldn't be drink-ing quite so fast. The phrase "Slow down there, partner, not all at once!" went through his head. For some reason, in old westerns they always said that to people as they drank for the first time after being res-cued from the desert. He didn't know why, but they always seemed to say that. He tried to slow down, but he just couldn't. It was a large can-teen, with what appeared to be close to a half-gallon capacity. Nathaniel was nearing the bottom when he stopped. "Are you sure you don't mind if I drink all of it?" he gasped between gulps.

"Go right ahead. Water's cheap and it sounds like you needed it."

Nathaniel was grateful and he was still thirsty. He felt that he could have downed another couple of quarts. When he finished what was left he set the canteen down where it had been. "Thank you, thank you very much," Nathaniel responded appreciatively, his voice returning.

He slowly made his way around the small fire and for the first time saw the man's face. He had a rather dark complexion, a great head with strong chiseled features, and a square jaw. It was difficult to guess his age, and at first glance Nathaniel might have said twenty-five. But the longer Nathaniel looked at him, the more he thought this could not be so, for the man's dark eyes looked so incredibly wise. "My name is Nathaniel O'Brien," he offered as he took one step to the side of the fire and extended his right hand.

The man looked into Nathaniel's face with what appeared to be almost a look of amusement. "My name is Ethan; good to meet you, Nathaniel." His extended his hand swallowed Nathaniel's.

"I don't know what I would have done if you hadn't come along. You see, last night I was taking a short cut through the composting area and somewhere along the way I got totally disoriented and I ended up here, wherever this is. I was very thirsty when I came upon this lake, so I started to drink out of it, but I became sick and I must have passed out. The next thing I knew I woke up here."

"That water is no good for drinking," Ethan declared.

"I know that now! I hope there isn't anything toxic in it that I need to worry about," Nathaniel said somewhat nervously as he looked over at the body of water for the first time in daylight. "Wow, this is a big lake! I didn't realize that there was a lake this large around here." The water extended as far as his eyes could see. As he looked down the shoreline, he saw that it was lined with tall, desolate cliffs. The only waters he could think of that had embankments that looked even vaguely similar were the Mississippi River or the St. Croix River, and they were miles away from where he lived. But as he studied the land-scape, it looked too dry and barren to be either. "I know that you can hardly go a mile without running into a lake in Minnesota, but I've lived around here most of my life, and I don't recall seeing one this large around here. What is its name?"

"It has different names. One name is Lake Asphaltitis."

"Lake Asphaltitis, Lake Asphaltitis," Nathaniel mused rubbing his chin. That name wasn't even remotely familiar. He wondered if this stranger might be pulling his leg, as he did seem to have a rather amused look on his face. But then again, he thought the taste of the lake did have all the qualities of asphalt. "I guess I've never heard of it."

"Most people call it the Dead Sea," Ethan added.

"After drinking from it, I can see why! " he proclaimed with a laugh. "Lake Asphaltitis, hmmm... Well, if that is the name of this lake, then I sure have wandered off. What in the world is in it anyway; do you know?"

"Oh, I hear it has a high sodium composition, although I have never drunk from it," Ethan conceded, looking even more amused.

"I didn't know we had any lakes like that around here," Nathaniel said, not quite sure what a lake with high sodium composition was but becoming slightly annoyed at what he considered Ethan's smug looks.

"You seem to be lost. If you'd like, I could give you some idea where you are. Tell me now. You don't really know where you are, do you?" Ethan finally asked him.

Nathaniel despised ever admitting that he was lost or needed directions. It always made him feel so vulnerable and not in control of the situation. "Well, of course I do. I mean, generally. I just got myself turned around a bit!" he retorted somewhat indignantly as he scanned the area.

"Then you know where you are?" Ethan queried with a raised eyebrow.

"Like I said, I just wandered off a bit; that's all. I wouldn't call that lost," Nathaniel snapped back. He was starting to feel a little testy because he was dirty, his head was full of sand, and of course, in reality he had no idea where he was. He was not in the mood to answer questions from some strange man on some strange beach. Besides, this robed gentleman seemed to be taking pleasure in discovering whether Nathaniel knew where he was, so Nathaniel was eager to redirect the conversation.

"I suppose it's none of my business, but I have been wondering what you are doing out here dressed like you are, in that… that… whatever it is you're wearing. Seems a rather odd way to be camping out. And I wouldn't imagine you caught those fish in that wretched lake, did you?" Nathaniel asked, pointing to the fish that were frying on the fire.

Ethan let out a deep hearty laugh "Now you're catching on, Nathaniel!" Nathaniel failed to see the humor in his question.

"You're right, I didn't catch these fish here. As for my outfit, well, I find it quite comfortable."

"Yeah, I suppose it's not easy finding clothes to fit a guy like you," Nathaniel quipped.

Ethan, who was still crouched by the fire, slowly rose. Higher and higher he seemed to go. When he finally stood erect, he was over eight feet tall.

"Oh boy," Nathaniel muttered in a weak, small voice and took a few steps backward.

"Say there, I didn't mean to frighten you," Ethan said with concern in his voice. "I guess I sometimes overlook what effect my size has on huma... people."

Nathaniel stood there dumbfounded, his mouth hanging open. He looked Ethan up and down a few times, not knowing what to do or say. He had never before come across anyone near such a tremendous size. It hardly seemed possible that a human could reach such colossal proportions.

Suddenly Nathaniel's eyes grew even wider, and his expression changed from astonishment to alarm; for he noticed what appeared to be the handle of a great sword protruding from underneath Ethan's robe. Nathaniel started to take a few more steps backward and was prepared to turn and run for he knew that even without the sword he would stand no chance defending himself against someone of Ethan's size.

Ethan's eyes caught Nathaniel's, and he suddenly realized what Nathaniel's gaze was fixed on. "Hold on, Nathaniel, relax! I see now that I will have to speak more directly. I regret any misunderstandings, but I'm sure that once I explain, you will see I had no choice. What has happened to you is something unusual and rare." Ethan looked down at the ground for a moment and seemed to be collecting his thoughts. Then, he looked deeply into Nathaniel's eyes and, smiling, said, "Where shall I start? Maybe it would be appropriate to begin with this quote." Ethan took a breath and began. 'What is man, that thou art mindful of him? And the son of man, that thou visited him? For thou hast made him a little lower than the angels, and hast crowned him with glory and honor.'"

Nathaniel didn't like the sound of this. He was now fairly sure that Ethan must be a mental case of some sort, a gargantuan madman walking around in the middle of nowhere dressed in a toga and carrying around what appeared to be a very large sword. The fact that Ethan now seemed to be speaking rather cryptically made it all the worse. Combine those elements together, and it didn't take a genius, Nathaniel thought, to realize it was time to leave.

"You know, I've enjoyed our time together, but it's time for me to be going. I've truly enjoyed your hospitality," he acknowledged, speaking in a calm and controlled voice. "Listen, I really appreciated the water. I hope you enjoy the fish. They look mighty good! Bon appétite!" Nathaniel was taking small steps backward as he spoke, and turned to walk away when he finished.

"But you don't have any idea where you're going," Ethan shouted to him.

"Oh, don't worry about me. I'll find my way. Thanks again!" Nathaniel yelled as he broke into a mild trot.

"Well, if you really must go, you will need this," Ethan shouted. Nathaniel turned and watched as Ethan picked up the canteen off the ground, and even though he was a already a good fifty yards away, with a flick of a powerful wrist, sent the canteen sailing through the air, landing it with a heavy thud at Nathaniel's feet.

"Thanks!" Nathaniel hollered back, seeing little need for the canteen now but deciding it would be better if he went along with the stranger's eccentricities. Nathaniel bent down and picked it up. "Oh, well, I was still thirsty anyway," he said to himself as he unscrewed the cap and brought the canteen to his lips. He began to walk away as he drank, again enjoying the refreshing water. It certainly quenched his thirst, he thought, but it couldn't compare to that first drink he had out of it, when he had such a horrible thirst, a thirst so great that he had drunk it dry.

Nathaniel suddenly stopped in his tracks as he realized the contradiction in his thought. He had seen Ethan pick up this same canteen that he had drunk dry, and now as he held it in his hands, it was heavy with water again! His mind went back over the strangeness of the last twelve hours—his truck going dead for no reason, the apparent transformation of the compost area, the wretched lake, the oddly dressed giant, and now this canteen.

"Care for some fish?" Ethan asked as Nathaniel neared the fire.

"I guess so… sure," he answered.

The fire crackled and snapped as the two sat there and ate. For a while, nothing was said. Nathaniel finally spoke, "Who are you?"

Ethan just stared at the flames. The reflection of the fire danced in his eyes.

"What's going on here? This whole thing has a surreal feeling about it. Somehow I think you know exactly what I mean. I've had some strange things happen to me since last night."

Ethan finally looked up with a smile. "I surmised it was better that you figure this out yourself than for me to try to convince you or chase after you when you were leaving. I'm sure I would have only scared you to death."

"Right. So… by that you mean that I'm not dead right now and this isn't the afterlife or anything like that?" Nathaniel questioned with a slightly shaky voice.

Ethan let out a deep and hearty laugh, "No! I should say not! You are certainly not dead!"

Nathaniel let go a sigh of relief, for the possibility most certainly had crossed his mind. "Well, if I'm not dead, then what's going on here and why is all this happening to me?"

Ethan poked at the fire with a stick.

"How have the last few weeks been going for you?" The look of amusement that Ethan had carried with him earlier had faded and he suddenly grew serious.

"This has something to do with Reverend McDermit, doesn't it?"

"Well, yes, to some degree. But more precisely, it is about you about some of the actions that you have taken and the attitudes you have displayed recently. Before I go any further, let me make one thing perfectly clear from the beginning. Only God knows your thoughts, Nathaniel, and unless he chooses to inform us, we angels can only go by our past experience with humans; although I must say our experience with mankind is very extensive. Myself, I have six thousand years of experience. I guess what I am trying to say is that I have been informed that you are on the verge of throwing away your faith and your relationship with God because of attitudes and behaviors you have observed in other people. Is that correct?"

"You… are you really are an angel?" Nathaniel blurted out in amazement. "No one else would have known I felt exactly that way. I can't believe that God would be this interested in me… but this is all real," he said grabbing a fistful of sand. "This is really happening." He looked over at Ethan and realized that he was waiting for an answer to his question. "Oh, yes, I'm sorry, I would say you summed it up quite nicely," he finally answered, feeling slightly embarrassed by his prattling.

"Good," stated Ethan, almost businesslike. "We will get on with it then."

"Get on with what?" Nathaniel asked.

"Pay attention now, Nathaniel, for my time with you is very short. You have been given an opportunity to see and encounter things that very few men have ever experienced. But, I also must tell you, that for unto whomsoever much is given, much will be required. Your heart is good, Nathaniel, and so is your resolution. That is why you were chosen, but you lack wisdom and understanding, attributes that you will sorely need now and in the future. You will learn much here, but most of what you are going to see and learn you must experience alone."

"I'm still not clear what you're talking about," Nathaniel interjected.

"Of course you're not, how could you? There are powers and principalities that influence your world that most humans either are not aware of, or don't believe in anymore." He paused for a moment, stroking his square jaw. "Your generation, for example," Ethan grimaced as the words crossed his lips, as though it pained him to utter them. He shook his head back and forth. "Your generation has produced the most arrogant and ignorant human beings ever to set foot on God's earth. Your technology—your cars, your computers, your music, your space travel, your medicines—deceives you. For men then say to themselves, 'Look at us, look at what we have done, we are in command of our lives, of our destinies. We are not like our ancestors, who needed to cling to God and superstition! Their morals and fears do not bind us, for we are wiser than they. We are in charge, we are in control!' But they are deceived and blind, and they begin to worship the creation rather than the creator. 'We will save the earth, we will love and cherish this planet, for it is ours and ours alone,' I hear them proclaim. Hah! Man can no more save the earth than he can destroy it. He is only its gardener, not its master! What a delusion he is under, how powerful he believes himself to be—as though he himself is God. Mankind's knowledge is still so infantile it's on the level of... how shall I put it?" Ethan thought for a moment. "Like a child discovering his toes, and even then I overestimate his comprehension. For when man disregarded the knowledge of God and his need for him, perfect knowledge became unattainable. Modern man makes the same mistake humans have always made, which renders them almost helpless against strong deception."

Ethan continued, "When people begin to place their faith in things other than God, be it education, knowledge, materialism, environmentalism, or even another person, they become blind and vulnerable, easy prey for the enemy. What has happened to your world is now happening to your churches. They ignore the spiritual forces that influence this planet. You are fighting a war, Nathaniel. Your pastor Reverend McDermit understood this very well. That is how he kept Mullyrug and his horde at bay for all those years. What a warrior your pastor was!"

"Mullyrug? Who or what is a Mullyrug?" Nathaniel questioned.

"Mullyrug," Ethan muttered, growling the word. "He is a deceiver, a manipulator. That is who he is! A whisperer, a wordbender, a betrayer! That is Mullyrug!" Ethan snarled, his eyes flashing as he repeated the name.

"He, my friend, is your real enemy. He had your church once. He thought he had a stranglehold on it, but it slipped out of his hands," Ethan said at the same time letting a handful of sand slip out between his thick fingers. "That Reverend McDermit! With the power of God flowing through him, he just marched right in and snatched that church away from Mullyrug. If you could have seen the look on Mullyrug's vile face! He spent the next forty years desperately looking for any crack that he and his army could slither back in through." Ethan was becoming more animated as he told the story.

"He finally found a way back in with Charlie Fitch. Charlie started out as a good man, but he had two weaknesses: pride, and lack of a consistent prayer life. Well, through his many channels, Mullyrug and those under him discovered this flaw and began their campaign on Charlie shortly after finding out that he was going to audition for the assistant pastor job at Mount Calvary Church. Charlie was an easy target for them. After a couple of years of working on him in Lexington, he was right where Mullyrug wanted him."

Nathaniel was following some of what Ethan was saying, but much of it he still found unclear.

"Mullyrug then sent for reinforcements, other creatures like him whose skills are whispering lies into men's ears. Soon the church was within his grasp again. It didn't take long for them to start planting the idea of having Reverend McDermit removed from the pastorate. With that now accomplished, Mullyrug will dig his heels in and again have a place to spread his deceptions, lies, and confusion."

"This Mullyrug... I take it then that he must be some sort of demon or spirit?" Nathaniel asked.

"That's right. Demon, spirit, shape-shifter, whatever you would like to call him. But Mullyrug and his ilk are all the same, all fallen angels who were at one time servants of the Lord. Oh, what they all threw away when they decided to follow the evil one!" Ethan's hands were clenched and he had a faraway look in his eyes. He sat there for a moment quietly, his eyes open but seeing something far away and long, long ago. Just when Nathaniel thought that maybe Ethan was waiting for him to respond, Ethan spoke. "Mullyrug... Mullyrug!" Ethan spoke the name with great contempt, as if he were trying to spew a foul tasting food from his mouth. "Why? Even now I ask myself, why? You took the wonderful name that God gave you and exchanged it for that of a demon, a name given to you by that wretched one! Why did you do it? We soared among the stars and the heavens together. We laughed and worshipped at the Father's feet. He gave us everything our hearts desired! If we had been human, we would have been closer than brothers. But you cast your lot with Lucifer. He would have corrupted me also if I had hesitated, if I had paused for a moment to listen. And then you were gone; cast out, and the great liar took a third of you with him!" he shouted, shaking his head sadly back and forth. Ethan's eyes were misty now, pain etched in his face. A lone tear broke from one eye and ran down the side of his face.

Nathaniel was stunned. "I… I'm sorry Ethan. I don't know what to say. I didn't realize that angels… er… that you could feel this way about things. I didn't even know angels could cry."

"Am I?" Ethan asked, feeling his face with his hand. "So I am. It's amazing… after all this time… it still hurts so deeply. My, but it's been ages since I last thought about this, at least thought about it so deeply. Maybe two or three hundred years," he disclosed, quickly regaining control of his emotions.

"No matter. My friend is dead now, and it is Mullyrug who is here. He and his cohorts are the real enemy. You must understand, Nathaniel, it is they who are responsible for the confusion in your world. It does no one any good if your anger and aggression are directed toward other people, the ones who are being manipulated. There are better ways."

"I'm sure there are," Nathaniel answered. "But what I don't understand is how foolish and gullible people are. Look at what Charlie Fitch and the people of Mount Calvary Church did. Right is right; wrong is wrong; isn't it? I know what you are getting at, Ethan. But Reverend McDermit gave his life to his congregation, and when he was no longer useful to them, they discarded him with little or no conscience. Is that what a Christian is? What a sad excuse for any human being, much less someone who would call themself a Christian. Are you saying then that every mistake we make, we can just explain it away by blaming it on the devil?"

"Oh, of course not, Nathaniel. But you underestimate your enemy. You, or any other humans, are simply no match for him. They are supernatural beings; you are not. If you become their target and are not prepared, they will eat you—eat you alive. You must recall that you were taught that the devil walks the earth like a lion, seeking whom he may devour. There is only one way that a human can defend himself from Satan."

"Yes, I know all those things. But what I still can't accept is that a whole church of Christians could all be deceived so easily. Why wasn't I fooled then?"

"Maybe because you knew Reverend McDermit better than most of them. People have strengths and weaknesses in different areas. But don't delude yourself, Nathaniel. You might find out that you are not the pillar of strength that you think you are."

Nathaniel felt his face turn warm with embarrassment. "I… never said I was a pillar of strength. I just meant it was a horrible thing they did, that there was no excuse for it."

"You're right, it was a horrible thing. We will agree on that," Ethan paused. "But it is just about time for you to go, so we must move on to other things," and with that, he pursed his lips and let out a loud whistle. He reached inside his white robe and pulled out a smaller, striped, brown robe, and he produced a pair of sandals from his outside pockets. "Here put these on," he ordered as he handed them to Nathaniel.

"Hawwwwwwwww! Heeeeeeee!"

Nathaniel, who had been sitting cross-legged on the ground was startled at the loud and unexpected noise that came from directly behind him. His hands flew up in the air and he fell over on to his back.

"Quiet, Khamore, quiet! Look what you have done to our friend here!" Ethan scolded as he pulled Nathaniel to his feet. Nathaniel turned and found himself staring into the face of an astonishingly homely mule. He was very dark and had loose, overly large lips like a camel's, wide flaring nostrils, and long ears that hung down on the sides of his head.

"Khamore will be your transportation while you are here. I have had a little talk with him, so he knows where to bring you. He is a good mule and knows the area very well. He belongs to the Essenes who live near here," Ethan explained as he stroked the animal's long nose.

"What do you mean? Where am I going that I would need one of these? You can tell Mr. Essene that Khamore's services won't be needed. I understand what you have been trying to tell me. My faith's been restored. Besides, why would I need a mule in Minnesota?"

"Minnesota? I'm sorry, Nathaniel. It seems that I haven't been paying enough attention. I thought that you had figured it out. You're no longer in Minnesota."

"I'm not?" Nathaniel questioned as he looked around. He began to feel apprehensive. "Where am I then?"

"Haven't you noticed how warm it's become, or the landscape? Is it usually this warm on an early April morning in Minnesota?" Ethan queried.

It did seem unusually warm right now, even hot, Nathaniel thought, but he still had no idea where he was. He was beginning to feel uneasy again about all of this. It seemed that every time he was getting his bearings, Ethan threw something new at him. "All right then, Ethan, where am I?"

"Do you remember when you asked me what lake this was, and I said that it was Lake Asphaltitis, but that some people call it the Dead Sea?"

"Yes."

"Well, that's what it is. It really is the Dead Sea. Lake Asphaltitis is a name the Romans gave it."

Nathaniel felt the blood rush from his head and everything begin to spin. He closed his eyes and let out a low moan. He didn't like this game any more. "The Dead Sea!" he thought to himself. "That was somewhere in the Middle East! What am I doing here?" He shouted at Ethan, "You mean to tell me that I am thousands of miles from my home? Aren't there terrorists and nomadic tribes around here? What if one of them decides to shoot me? They always seem to be shooting someone in these parts!"

"Relax, no one is going to shoot you. I guarantee it. You see, we are standing on the west side of the Dead Sea as it was long, long ago. Nathaniel, the Essenes are a reclusive people, a Jewish sect who live near here and who have been kind enough to lend us the services of one of their mules. Khamore will take you out of here on a little-known path up the sides of the cliffs. It's terribly steep and full of crevices and ravines, but Khamore is a good climber. He will lead you to Hyrcania, which years ago was a fortress but is now a decrepit prison. I would advise you not to stop there. Use it for a reference point only, because it is a violent, wicked place. From there you will take the road to Bethany, which is about seven miles from Hyrcania. You should arrive there by evening, and you will stay the night and then early the next morning travel to Jerusalem. Keep to yourself. When you find it necessary to come in contact with others, reveal little or nothing about yourself. It is better that way. You will be travelling on a fairly steep, uphill grade the entire time, as the Dead Sea is the lowest place on earth. It is still spring, so even though the desert is hot, it is endurable. In the pockets of your robe you will find a small pouch that contains enough money for your food and lodging. You also have a sack filled with water."

"What do you mean I'm at the Dead Sea as it was long, long ago? Are you talking about some sort of time travel here? Why do I need to do this? Can't you explain a little more to me?" Nathaniel protested as he slipped the robe on and began taking off his shoes.

"The time is not right, Nathaniel. You will discover many of the answers you seek on your own. You need to be on your way," Ethan said, motioning for Nathaniel to get up onto the mule. But the only pony riding Nathaniel had ever done was on a merry-go-round horse, and he eyed the animal apprehensively. "Shouldn't he have a saddle or something?"

Ethan chuckled, "Oh, I think that the blanket on his back will do just fine. Come on now, up you go," he said as he grabbed Nathaniel by the upper arm, lifting him in the air like a child and placing him on the mule. He gave it a slap, and said, "To Bethany, Khamore, to Bethany!"

Khamore bellowed and started toward a path fifty yards away. Nathaniel frantically grabbed the reigns and bounced up and down on the mule's back. "W–wh–at–t d–do I–I d–do in-n J–Jer–rusal–lem?" he shouted back to Ethan. Ethan said nothing and just smiled and waved. Nathaniel turned back to look, but Ethan was gone.

"Oh, great, out in the middle of nowhere all alone!" Nathaniel grumbled to himself as he bounced along the trail.

But he wasn't alone. For not far from where he and Ethan had been talking, a dark figure stepped out from behind a large rock, its yellow eyes following him closely.

CHAPTER NINE

Unexpected Strangers

Nathaniel walked and climbed much of the time as he and Khamore slowly made their way to the top of the cliffs. The view of the Dead Sea from there was breathtaking. A bluish haze hung over the surface of the water, the bright colors in sharp contrast to the brown and white sand surrounding it. The desert in front of him was devoid of any green, resembling a lunar landscape. It was a barren land with great rolling hills of sand. The air seemed to be getting hotter by the minute as the morning sun rose in the sky.

"I hope you really know where you are going," Nathaniel said nervously to Khamore. Khamore grunted. They traveled for some time up and down the steep hills and crevices, until in the distance Nathaniel finally spotted what appeared to be a small walled city. "That must be Hyrcania. Is that Hyrcania, Khamore?" Nathaniel asked, patting the side of Khamore's neck. The mule ignored the question and plodded on.

Mindful of Ethan's warning about Hyrcania, Nathaniel had no desire to venture any closer. But when he was within a few hundred yards, he noticed a lone figure sitting on the ground outside the walls. The man began to call and motion to Nathaniel. "What should we do, Khamore, what should we do? Ethan told us not to get to close to this place." The man continued to call and move his arms around, motioning them to come nearer.

"Well, I suppose I better see what he wants. Maybe he needs some help." As Nathaniel got closer, he noticed that the man held what looked to be a wine sack in one hand. The man struggled to his feet and then fell over. He appeared to be some type of guard, because on his chest was a metal breastplate; but his clothes were ragged and old, his hair and beard unkempt. Nathaniel was only about twenty yards away when the man grabbed a large spear that was lying next to him, planted in the ground, and used it to pull himself up. It was obvious he was quite inebriated. He motioned for Nathaniel to come closer.

"Is this Hyrcania?" Nathaniel queried.

The man appeared puzzled by the question. He mumbled something unintelligible to Nathaniel and motioned for him to get off Khamore. "Tis eisi humas?" he snarled at Nathaniel.

Nathaniel dismounted and looked blankly back at him, having no idea what he had said or what he wanted. The man sneered at Nathaniel and started to take a wobbly step toward him, when he glanced over at Khamore. A look of amusement quickly came to his face. "Humas eisi heis bdeo hippos!" he exclaimed and began to laugh. He totally ignored Nathaniel, walked over to Khamore and stood nose-to-nose with him. "Humas eisi heis bdeo hippos!" he reiterated, and began to laugh harder. Translated, he was stating that Khamore was one "very ugly horse." Whatever it was the man was drinking from his wine sack made it all the more amusing to him.

The longer the man stared into at the face of the mule, who stared back at him, the harder he began to laugh. Tears began to run down his face and he began to hold his stomach. He turned his back on Khamore and Nathaniel and began shouting toward the wall, for he wanted one of his friends to come and take a look at the funny-looking beast.

Khamore, despite his looks, was a sensitive animal and didn't appreciate being the object of this man's laughter. While the man's back was turned, Khamore came forward, pulled back his impressive lips, and sunk his teeth deep into the man's backside. The man threw back his head and howled in pain. Nathaniel stood there for an instant, stunned because it all had happened so fast. He quickly regained his senses and leapt onto the back of Khamore. The mule let out a bellow of triumphant proportions and galloped away (as fast as a mule can gallop), with Nathaniel bouncing up and down on his back.

The guard began to sink to his knees, but as he was going down, he suddenly whirled around and hurled his spear at them. Fortunately, whatever he had been drinking had impaired him enough so that the weapon sailed harmlessly wide of its mark. Soon Nathaniel and Khamore were safely past the fortress and on the main road to Bethany.

The terrain was still full of large cracks and crevices, but the drop-offs were not so dramatic. Nathaniel wondered what time it was. He hadn't eaten since Wednesday, and his stomach began to make noises about it. Nathaniel searched in the large pockets of the robe to see if Ethan had left anything in there. His fingers discovered something rough and stiff, and he pulled it out to inspect it. He held up seven or eight pieces of what appeared to be dried hunks of meat. He sniffed at it and bit off a small piece. "Not bad," he declared out loud. "A little chewy, but I can't complain. Thanks, Ethan, wherever you are," he said while saluting into the air.

The sun was beginning to beat down on Nathaniel's head and neck, so he pulled up his hood. He took a drink from his sack and continued on, traveling for several hours on Khamore before deciding to dismount. He was not used to riding and was becoming stiff and sore. Besides, he did not want to overwork Khamore, for Nathaniel knew they had a long way to go. He peered west as far as he could, hoping to see something—anything—but large rolling mounds of sand. Suddenly he did see something. Far away—two, no, three dots coming over a hill. Up the road they came and soon disappeared again behind another mound a long way off. Nathaniel's first reaction was excitement. But that was soon tempered by the thought that he was not sure who or what would be travelling this way across this forsaken land in the middle of the day. Nevertheless, he struggled to get his sore body back on Khamore and trotted forward.

It was another half-hour until he could vaguely make out the figures who were making their way toward him. The dots became two men leading by a rope what appeared to be a large dog. Soon the two men were within shouting distance. As they approached Nathaniel, they were waving and all smiles. "This is more like it," thought Nathaniel.

As they drew closer, Nathaniel could see that what he thought was a large dog was really a small sickly looking donkey, and an overloaded one at that. The dark, bearded men looked very poor and thin. The fabric of their robes was faded and worn. One man wore a patch over one eye and carried a large shepherd's staff; the other man, who was shorter, was missing two of his fingers on his right hand. When the men greeted Nathaniel, they enthusiastically threw their arms around him and embraced him. Nathaniel felt them lightly running their hands up and down his arms and chest and waist, and they then kissed him on the cheek like a long-lost brother. They were both missing most of their teeth, and their breath was so rancid it made Nathaniel eyes water. They, like the guard he had met earlier, spoke in a tongue that Nathaniel couldn't understand.

The two men, after realizing that Nathaniel did not speak their language, began focusing their attention on Khamore. They circled around him, patting him on the back and chattering back and forth. The man with the eye patch stroked Khamore's face. He lifted up Khamore's lips and began to inspect his teeth. Satisfied, he nodded to the other man, who went over to their donkey, pulled it over to Nathaniel by its rope, placing the rope in Nathaniel's hand. The two of them then began to unload their belongings off their donkey and arranging it on Khamore's back.

"Hey, wait a minute! What do you think you're doing!? I'm not about to make a trade like that!" Nathaniel shouted as he dropped the rope and ran over to the two men.

He was running past the man with the eye patch and about to try to stop the shorter man from placing anything else on Khamore when he felt a staff shoot between his feet. He tumbled to the ground in a cloud of dust and sand. Khamore seemed to understand what was going on and suddenly sat down, spilling the unsecured belongings of the two men onto the ground.

The three-fingered man stepped in front of Khamore and began yelling and motioning at him to stand up. The one-eyed man with the staff walked quickly past Nathaniel, but not before giving him a solid rap on the head with the stick. For a moment, everything went black in Nathaniel's head and stars moved across his eyes. The man with the staff was now behind Khamore and began to laugh and kick Khamore on his back end. The three-fingered man attempted to grab Khamore by the head and pull forward, but Khamore grunted and shook his head back and forth defiantly, resisting him. The man with the staff let out a sadistic laugh as he watched his friend's struggle. He finally called out to the shorter man, who then gave up his wrestling match with Khamore. The one-eyed man had a wicked grin on his face and now held the staff over his shoulder with both hands. He lifted the staff above his head and struck Khamore hard on the back. Khamore raised his head to the sky and brayed mournfully.

Nathaniel had been lying somewhat dazed on the ground. But the sight of the man beating Khamore and the animal's cry of pain revitalized him. The man raised his stick preparing a second blow, when, with anger and rage surging through him, Nathaniel jumped to his feet and sprinted at him, driving his shoulder and sturdy frame into his adversary's chest. The thief had been so consumed with beating Khamore that he was caught totally off guard. His staff went sailing into the air as the full force of Nathaniel's body slammed into his thin frame. Nathaniel's momentum sent both of them crashing to the ground, with the one-eyed man landing on his back, Nathaniel atop him. The thief's body absorbed most of the violent concussion. His back arched and his one eye bulged as he began gasping for air, for the impact had knocked the wind out of him. Nathaniel turned quickly and saw the three-fingered man rushing toward him. He pushed himself off the thief on the ground and after two strides threw himself sideways at the rushing man's legs, knocking them out from under him. Nathaniel rolled cleanly past him and the man fell face first into the road.

Nathaniel jumped to his feet and then walked over to the two battle-weary men on the ground. "Take your things and get out of here!"

he screamed angrily at them while motioning toward the bags in the road. He wiped the sweat from his face with his sleeve.

The two men knew very well what Nathaniel was saying and slowly got to their feet. Holding his injured face, the three-fingered man began to walk over to their belongings, while the other took a couple of steps to retrieve his staff. Nathaniel cut in front of him, "No way, that stays here." Nathaniel had been in many altercations in his life, so he was experienced in measuring another man's strengths and weaknesses. The resistance his body felt when he plowed into both of them told him that they were no match for him physically. Nathaniel felt confident that without the staff in their possession, he could handle both men.

The one-eyed thief didn't seem tremendously upset about not being able to retrieve his staff and limped over to his friend. They had their backs turned to Nathaniel as they gathered up their things around Khamore. Suddenly, they both turned around, and in their hands were large knives that they had concealed in their bags. They knew he was defenseless, for they had made a quick search to see if he was carrying any valuables or weapons on his body when they had greeted him.

The wicked toothless grin returned to the man who had been carrying the staff. They had caught Nathaniel totally unprepared and quickly got on both sides of him, poking at and taunting at him. They were close enough that Nathaniel, if he had tried to run, would probably get a knife in the back for his efforts. The two seemed to be enjoying the sadistic game, coming inches from Nathaniel's arms and face as he jumped back and forth.

Suddenly, Nathaniel saw the three-fingered man's face grow very serious. The thief's eyes grew larger as he took a few steps backward and dropped his weapon. The one-eyed man scowled at his accomplice, admonishing him to pick up his knife. The three-fingered man shook his head, whispering something under his breath as he pointed a bony finger at something behind the man with the eye patch. The one-eyed thief stared at the three-fingered thief with a look of confusion on his face. Nathaniel slowly turned his head and glanced over his shoulder, as did the man with the knife. There, standing in front of the sun stood a massive figure over eight feet tall.

Nathaniel squinted his eyes trying to make out the figure standing in the sunlight. "Ethan!" Nathaniel shouted.

The man with the knife gasped and dropped it onto the road. "Leave, the both of you, now!" The booming voice commanded. They frantically scrambled about, loading up their things in their arms and running over to their donkey.

"No, leave that pitiful animal alone! Leave, I said!" the voice ordered. The two men nodded their heads in compliance and fell over themselves as they headed east down the road in the direction they had been going.

"Ethan, am I ever thankful that you showed up! I think they would have tired of their game soon and who knows what they would have done then!" Nathaniel exclaimed gratefully, thoroughly soaked from head to toe with perspiration. Nathaniel moved to one side so that the sun did not obscure his view of Ethan. As Ethan's features became clear, he was startled to discover that it was, in fact, not Ethan at all! Although in many ways they were very similar in appearance, this angel's hair was blonde, his features not quite as rugged, and he wore a beautiful flowing purple cape attached to his white robe.

"You look exhausted, my friend! I'm glad I was here to aid you when you needed it. But as you can see, I am not Ethan. My name is Bartholomew. Ethan sent me to watch over you while he was occupied with some other matters," he explained as he extended his hand.

"Oh… well, thank you anyway!" Nathaniel gushed, grinning ear to ear, shaking Bartholomew's large hand.

"I warn you, I can't stay long. As you may have noticed, we angels are a busy lot. But I suppose I can spend a few moments with you before I leave, if you like."

"By all means. I don't think I will ever be too busy to turn down fellowship with an angel," Nathaniel joked.

"What a delightful sense of humor! No wonder Ethan enjoys talking to you so much!"

"He said that?" Nathaniel asked, feeling flattered.

"Well, of course he did!" replied Bartholomew. He walked over to the sickly looking donkey and stroked its head. Its dull coat immediately began to shine and it seemed to grow fat and healthy before Nathaniel's eyes. "I despise it when people abuse animals, don't you?" Bartholomew casually asked.

"Amazing!" declared an astonished Nathaniel.

"What do you mean…? Oh, you mean the donkey. Yes, I guess to a human, it would be considered a miracle. Sometimes I hardly realize what I've done. This is nothing really."

"Really?" inquired an astonished Nathaniel.

"Oh, of course not, my friend! Let me think. Well, I could.… Oh no, I really shouldn't. We really are not suppose to do this type of thing."

"What? What were you thinking about doing?" Nathaniel questioned excitedly.

"No, I'm sorry, the donkey was an accident."

"Oh… well, I'm sure there are restrictions about things like that," replied Nathaniel solemnly, as if he knew of such matters.

"Yes, there are; indeed there are." Bartholomew paused for a moment as he sensed Nathaniel's disappointment. Then a twinkle came to his eye. "You were eating something awhile back. May I see it?"

Nathaniel reached into his pocket and pulled out a stick of dried meat, "You mean this?"

"Yes, that's it," he said taking it from Nathaniel.

He pulled his cape forward in front of his body and placed the hand holding the dried beef inside it. He pulled it back out, and sitting on a shiny silver tray was a plate full of the best looking meat Nathaniel had ever seen. "I really should not have done this, but seeing that you're out in the middle of nowhere… well, I hope you enjoy it." He handed the plate to Nathaniel, who took a shiny silver fork from the tray and began to eat. "Delicious! This is the most succulent piece of meat I've had in my life!" Nathaniel wondered why Ethan couldn't have given him something better then a dried up piece of meat.

"Thank you!" Bartholomew enthusiastically responded. "How

courteous and cultured you are! You compliment that wonderful name of yours!"

"Really?" Nathaniel replied, flattered. "Which name do you mean— Nathaniel or O'Brien?" He queried between mouthfuls.

"Nathaniel, of course, Nathaniel! It means "the gift"! Didn't you know that?"

"No, I guess I didn't. The gift, you say?" Nathaniel was really beginning to like Bartholomew, the meat more than satisfied his hunger, and somehow he found this angel much more engaging and uplifting than Ethan.

"So, Nathaniel, on your way to Jerusalem, are you?"

"Yes, I am. You don't happen to know what this is all about do you? Ethan seemed so tight-lipped about it."

"Well, Nathaniel, much as I would like to tell you, I am not at liberty to say; but I do know that we hope there will be some very interesting things happening there very soon," he remarked with a smile.

"Is that right? Well, I suppose I better keep moving then. I've a few more miles to go."

"Oh, don't worry about that, Nathaniel. If nothing else, I can bring you there in a matter of a moment, in the blink of an eye, really."

"You mean to tell me it was unnecessary for me to travel by mule all this way, through this heat and the desert?" Nathaniel asked, somewhat incredulously.

"Well… I suppose other forms of transportation could have been arranged. I hesitated to tell you, since this is Ethan's assignment after all. Forgive me if…"

"No, think nothing of it," Nathaniel stated, interrupting Bartholomew in midsentence. "Maybe I shouldn't say this, but I only wish now, after meeting you, that it had been arranged so that you were my escort—if that's the word for whatever you angels are doing for me." Nathaniel finished his last bite of food and handed the tray back to Bartholomew.

"What a remarkably kind thing to say! Is it any wonder you are so well thought of! Since you now have more time than you thought, why don't we sit down? You seem to be such a fascinating human. You know, we angels rarely get a chance to actually converse with humans!" Bartholomew proclaimed as he walked over to a mound of sand and sat down.

"I don't know… Ethan told me I should… "

"Of course he did, but are you forgetting, Ethan told me that I was in charge until he returned? But if you insist, feel free to… " the angel said as he began to rise to his feet.

"I suppose you're right, Bartholomew, I don't even know why I'm arguing with you!" Nathaniel declared throwing his hands in the air and laughing.

"Running into some difficulties, Nathaniel?" a deep voice asked behind him. Startled, Nathaniel jumped a good half-foot into the air and whirled around.

"Ethan, what are you doing here?" Nathaniel inquired sheepishly, trying to recall the comments he had made earlier about Ethan.

"The question is, Nathaniel, what are you doing here? You should be on your way to Bethany. Weren't my instructions sufficient?"

"Well, of course they were, Ethan, but you see, I was attacked by these two men, and Bartholomew here saved me, and…"

"What manner of deceit and trickery have you been up to now?" Ethan shouted past Nathaniel.

"Deceit? Me?" Bartholomew asked incredulously, pointing to himself after each proclamation. "Why Ethan, you can't be serious. Can't you see, I'm an angel of the Lord! How dare you!" His words showed great offense at the accusations. But his response was a mockery, for when Nathaniel glanced again at Bartholomew, he saw a sneer creep across his lips.

"A demon? That's not what they look like… He saved my life, Ethan!" Nathaniel cried out.

"Who do you think sent them your way!" Bartholomew shouted, referring to the two thieves. He laughed a wicked laugh. "Who is this human, Ethan, I demand to know! He speaks strangely, not with the tongue of anyone native to this land! You know that we are well aware of every wretched human that walks the earth. Yet, neither I nor my servants know anything about him, which is impossible," the demon roared, leaping to his feet. Nathaniel felt his heart race and he stepped backward toward Ethan.

"When he revealed his name to me, it meant nothing," Bartholomew continued, shouting even louder. "He is not one of the chosen people—the way he devoured the pig I offered him told me that much. And if he is one of the chosen, he has broken the law and must be punished. You yourself know that much. I asked myself, 'Why does Ethan have an interest in this one? Why? Who is he and what is he doing here?' I demand to know who he is, Ethan! It is my right! I demand to know!" he screamed, as step by step he came closer. His eyes were becoming bloodred, his face full of rage.

Nathaniel was shaking with fear, for he had never seen such a terrifying sight in his life. He could feel a sudden chill in the air and a gloomy darkness seemed to come out of nowhere.

"Stand behind me, Nathaniel." Ethan ordered. Nathaniel darted behind him as Ethan drew his sword and stepped forward. Bartholomew's sword was ready and raised above his head. With a terrible scream, he came running forward and swung downward at Ethan. Ethan blocked it by holding his sword sideways above his head. Again and again Bartholomew swung his sword with unbridled rage, but Ethan's blade was always there to meet it. Bartholomew finally let out a bloodcurdling shriek of frustration and slammed his sword into a nearby rock. The stone exploded into small pieces on impact.

"So, have you had enough, Mullyrug?" Ethan calmly asked.

"Mullyrug?" whispered an astonished Nathaniel.

CHAPTER TEN

A Lesson Learned

"I demand to know who he is!" Mullyrug roared, pointing his sword at Nathaniel.

"You will make no demands around me, or around this man! Do you understand? Speak to me no longer of your rights, demon, for you will bother this one no more! You have meddled where you should not have meddled. You have tried my patience. Provoke me no longer!" Ethan's voice sounded like thunder, and the ground seemed to shake beneath Nathaniel's feet.

"I demand to…"

"Shall I call upon the name of the Lord? Shall I call down his holy power on your wickedness?" Ethan bellowed and began walking toward Mullyrug, his sword beginning to glow a brilliant white.

"No! Please, no!" Mullyrug abruptly cried out in a sad, weepy voice, his ferocity instantly vanishing. "Ethan, I beg of you, have mercy on me, do not torment me! Do you not recall you were once as my brother? Have mercy on me, my friend, my dear beloved friend, my merciful and righteous Ethan! Compassion! Have pity, I beg of you!" Mullyrug fell to the ground sobbing, his face in his hands as he became a whimpering ball of cowardice.

"Rise then," Ethan commanded.

When Mullyrug removed his hands from his face and rose to his feet, Nathaniel gasped. For the body that Mullyrug had appeared in was gone, dissolved like a vapor into the air. What stood before them now was an unbelievably wretched-looking creature. His face was almost serpentine in appearance. His eyes were like those of a snake, yellow with gray oval pupils; he had two slits where a nose should be, which sat on a protruding mouth and jaw. His robe was no longer white. It was now black with two reptilian hands sticking out of its baggy sleeves. The powerful-looking figure that had stood before them only moments before was gone, replaced by a grotesque and pathetic-looking creature that stood barely five feet tall.

"In the name of the Holy One, begone, demon, and bring your conspirator with you!" Ethan boldly ordered.

Mullyrug went over to the small donkey and hissed at it in a guttural language Nathaniel couldn't understand. Its physical appearance dissolved into vapor, and in its place stood a creature somewhat like Mullyrug, only smaller and naked. They both then dissolved into nothingness.

Khamore struggled to his feet and walked over to Ethan, nuzzling his head against his hand, grunting softly. "Well, hello there, Khamore. Did you miss me?" Ethan intoned as he bent down and stroked Khamore's head and long ears.

Nathaniel did not know what to say. He was ashamed that he had been misled so easily, so he stood behind Ethan's back for quite some time without saying a word.

"Nathaniel, have you gone?" Ethan called out, a hint of a smile on his face.

"Ah, no, I'm right here," he mumbled quietly.

"Don't feel too bad, Nathaniel, you were no match for the forces of darkness. That is what I was trying to explain to you before. I didn't want to go into too many details, for I knew Mullyrug was not far off."

An uncomfortable feeling began to settle in the pit of Nathaniel's stomach "You mean Mullyrug was back there with us at the Dead Sea?"

"Yes. But we are dealing with the Mullyrug of long ago, years before you were ever born. That is why he was so puzzled, and also why he was so furious; he had no record of you. The knowledge the enemy has on humans is utterly and thoroughly complete; that is their strength. Everyone is accounted for. They painstakingly chart and document every possible flaw or weakness they find in each mortal in hopes that it can be used against them at one time or another. They love to remind you all of your past failings. That is why he was in such a frenzy: because he knew nothing about you. You are from the future so he could report nothing to his master. You see, after studying you for a while and observing you on the road toward Jerusalem, Mullyrug sent one of his servants into the city in the form of a donkey. He purposely had those two pathetic thieves come across it shortly before they were ordered out of the city."

"Then he didn't even know my name to begin with, did he? He cleverly pulled it from me by flattery, telling me how wonderful it was!" Nathaniel voiced in amazement.

"Think, Nathaniel. How long were you with him?"

"Not long—maybe twenty minutes."

"Yet, wouldn't you say that in just that short amount of time, he had you eating out of the palm of his hand?"

"Literally," Nathaniel replied meekly, remembering the plate of pork.

"At first he called himself Bartholomew. Was that his name when you knew him? When he was an angel?" Nathaniel questioned Ethan somewhat hesitantly, for he remembered how painful it had been for Ethan to talk about.

"Yes, yes it was. When you first saw him Mullyrug appeared as he originally was, before he and the other angels followed Lucifer and were driven from heaven. You see, that is when demons are most effective, when they come as angels of light. Lucifer is the father of lies and of all false things from the beginning of time, from Nimrod to your generation. He blends enough truth into his deceptions that they become palatable for humans to swallow. That is why every spirit must be tested and tried, every doctrine submerged into the searing heat of truth, which is God's word, so no impurities remain."

Nathaniel suddenly felt overwhelmed. He had been easy prey.

"You don't understand. I have been trying my best, and look at how quickly and easily I was deceived! I can't live up to God's expectations. Send me home, Ethan. You have the wrong man. Whatever it is I'm supposed to do or learn, it's no use, I'm not the person you think I am."

Ethan chuckled, "Don't despair, Nathaniel. Your education has barely begun."

CHAPTER ELEVEN

Peculiar People

"I must be on my way again, Nathaniel. Down the road you will find a small bubbling spring from an underground stream. You will have to go off the main path to find it, but Khamore knows where it is. Let Khamore drink his fill, and refill your sack if need be," Ethan instructed as he walked with Nathaniel.

"You just got here. Do you really have to go—right now? Can't you walk with me at least until I reach Bethany?" Nathaniel pleaded. "This land is so lonely and desolate."

"No, that is not possible. But before I go, I will give you a gift."

Ethan stopped and turned to face Nathaniel. The angel placed his hands on Nathaniel's ears and said, "Let your ears be opened and let them hear." He placed his fingers on Nathaniel's eyes and said, "Let your eyes see clearly the things that are unseen." Lastly, he placed two fingers on Nathaniel's lips. "Let the bonds of Babel be released, let your words be understood."

Nathaniel looked at Ethan.

"What happened? I didn't feel anything. Was I supposed to feel something?"

"Travel on, Nathaniel, travel on," Ethan exhorted. His image then began to fade and soon there was nothing left of where he had been.

"Oh no, don't do this to me again! Come back!" Nathaniel shouted into an empty desert.

Nathaniel stood motionless for a moment, thinking about what had just transpired. He sighed and then cleared his throat.

"Hello, hello, hello," he said out loud as one might test a microphone.

"Hmmmph… I don't sound any different. I'm not quite sure what he did."

Nathaniel resigned himself to the fact that Ethan was gone, struggled onto Khamore's back, and again headed for Bethany. They traveled for another hour and Khamore found his way to the spring where both of them drank liberally and Nathaniel filled his container. Mile after slow rugged mile they plodded, making their way through the unforgiving terrain. The heat was starting to bother Nathaniel, and he nervously nudged Khamore onward as he watched the sun ride lower in the sky. Khamore grunted and tried to pick up the pace.

The clip-clop of Khamore's hoofs went on and on. Then on the horizon, Nathaniel saw it, a clump of white in the distance. He could see the village of Bethany.

"We made it! We made it!" he shouted to Khamore as he patted the side of the mule's head. They were still a good hour away, but just the sight of the city excited him. Khamore seemed to sense the nearness of the city and let out a happy snort.

When Nathaniel finally reached the edge of the city, the daylight was soon to be overcome by dusk. Although much of the land still appeared too desolate for his liking, he now saw patches of green—bushes and an assortment of trees. His journey through the wasteland nearing an end, Nathaniel began to realize how incredibly weary he was. The construction work he did was strenuous, but it couldn't compare to hiking miles through a sweltering desert, even if he had been on the back of a mule much of the way. His back and legs ached and it felt like the skin on his thighs had been rubbed raw from riding.

He could see children playing some type of game in an open field as he approached Bethany. They appeared to range in ages from eight to eleven years old, and he could hear their laughing and shrieking as they chased each other back and forth, using up every last moment of daylight. It was a wonderful sound to hear after having traveled through such a desolate place. It sounded almost musical, it was so happy, and also so normal. He badly needed to encounter something normal, considering the last twenty-four hours of his life.

"You did not touch me. You weren't even close!" Nathaniel heard a little girl shout as he came closer.

"I did too! I touched your sleeve!" another girl protested.

"You have to touch the person, not the clothes!" another added.

"The way I always played, touching the person or the clothes was good enough," Nathaniel commented as he slid off Khamore's back and approached the children.

The group of children suddenly grew quiet and turned to stare at the stranger.

"Who are you?" one of them finally grew brave enough to ask.

"My name is Nathaniel," he told them. His answer brought nothing but more silence. "Don't any of you talk?" he finally asked.

"I have an Uncle Nathaniel," one of them offered.

"Well, I have a brother Nathaniel," countered another.

"I have a cousin named Nathaniel," bragged yet another.

"Well, it looks like that's a popular name here!" Nathaniel exclaimed.

"Are you a son of Abraham and a son of David?" a little boy asked.

"Yes... yes, I suppose you could say that, in a matter of speaking," Nathaniel speculated, chuckling to himself. Suddenly his face lit up. "Wait a minute! I understand what you are saying, and you understand me!" he announced excitedly. "I imagine none of you speak English, am I right?"

"What is En...lish?" one of them asked.

"Amazing!" Nathaniel shouted. "So that's what Ethan did to me! I can understand their language and they can understand me!"

The children stood staring at him, puzzled by his words and actions. Finally, one of the two girls who had been arguing about the rules of the chase game whispered into another girl's ear and pushed her forward. "My sister Mary wants to know where you came from, and she also says you are very handsome!" she giggled.

Mary's face turned red with embarrassment as the other children burst out laughing. "I never said that Rebecca! Rebecca, you tell the truth, I did not say that!"

"She didn't actually say it, but I could tell that's what she was thinking!" Rebecca finally admitted.

"Well," Nathaniel said, "as far as where I am from, I'm originally from a place west of here, far, far away."

"Not from Rome, I hope!" one of the boys shouted.

"Not, I'm certainly not from Rome."

"Good!" answered the boy. "We hate the Romans here!"

"Jason, you know we're not supposed to hate people, not even the Romans! Don't you remember what Jesus said?" Mary scolded.

"I know what he said, but my father and mother have told me not to listen to him, because they don't believe he is the Messiah anymore."

Nathaniel gasped, "What do you mean, Jason, that you're not to listen to him anymore? You speak as though you have actually seen him, as though he is alive now."

"Well, of course he's alive, I just saw him yesterday, with his followers."

Nathaniel knelt down and placed his hand gently on Mary's shoulder. "Mary, this Jesus, have you seen him too?"

"Yes, almost everybody here has seen him." The other children nodded their heads in agreement.

"Are you sure? Do they call him the Christ? Is he a carpenter from Nazareth?"

"Yes, that's what they say. Why do you want to know? Are you looking for him?" Mary asked.

Tears filled Nathaniel's eyes, "Yes… I guess you could say that." Even though he had heard it with his own ears, he could still hardly believe it. What a gift he had been given! So now he finally knew what this was all about. He would be able to see Jesus Christ, possibly meet him face to face. Oh, the many questions he could ask! He didn't know how or why he had been granted this opportunity, but he was just grateful that it was happening.

"Thank you, thank you, children," he said softly, rising to his feet and wiping his eyes. He was very tired and hungry and the sun was all but gone. He knew that he still had to find a place to sleep.

"Could you direct me to an inn around here, where I could stay the night?"

"If you follow this road into the middle of the village, you will see a large rock, about as tall as you," one of the older boys explained. "When you come to the rock, go north down a narrow road. There is an inn there, about three buildings down. You'll know which one it is because there are a group of stables attached to it."

"Maaaaary… Rebeeeeeecca…!" The sound of a mother's voice drifted out into the field.

"We have to go now," Rebecca announced. "Good-bye, Nathaniel!"

"Good-bye and thank you, children. Good-bye Mary."

Mary blushed and quietly said, "Good-bye." She then turned and ran to catch up with her sister. The other children also turned to leave. Nathaniel grabbed Khamore's reigns and led him down the road toward the inn.

Bethany was a small village, so Nathaniel soon found the rock the boy had told him about, and from there followed the narrow road to the inn. He placed Khamore in a stall, filled a nearby bucket with water from a trough and set it in front of the mule. Khamore eagerly began drinking from the bucket while Nathaniel grabbed two armfuls of hay and placed that in front of him also. "That should hold you for awhile. I'm not really sure how much you need to eat or drink, but that should do until tomorrow. I've got to get some sleep. I'm exhausted," he muttered as he patted Khamore on the side and made his way to the innkeeper's door.

"Welcome, my friend, to the finest inn in Bethany!" a plump, middle-aged man greeted Nathaniel as he came through the door. The innkeeper had a receding hairline and a good day's growth of dark stubble on his face.

"I would like a room please," Nathaniel replied wearily. His energy was all but depleted now, and he was ready to fall asleep in the man's doorway.

"Well, come in, come in. You look ready for a good night's rest, and let me assure you, you have found it! Nothing in Jerusalem can compare to what you will find here. We are well known for our hospitality in these parts," he exclaimed. The innkeeper babbled on and on. He was very animated and seemed to take pride in telling Nathaniel every detail of the finer aspects of his place. All Nathaniel wanted to do was lie down.

He finally had to interrupt. "Excuse me sir, but I just want a place to sleep. Can you please give me a room?" He hadn't meant to, but the stress of his trip and his fatigue made the words leave his mouth gruffly.

The smile fell from the man's face. He had been cut off in mid-sentence, which displeased him greatly, for he was the type of man who found great pleasure listening to his own orations. "Certainly, sir," he snorted. "Since you are a stranger, I will require the money for the room beforehand."

"That's fine," Nathaniel answered nodding his head. He reached into the pocket of his robe for the money sack Ethan had given him, but he found nothing.

"One moment," he nervously said to the man, forcing a smile on his face. He checked his other pocket. Nothing but fragments of dried meat. The two thieves he had met on the road had cleverly stolen his money when they had embraced him.

"I'm sorry, sir, I seem to have misplaced my money. Would it be possible to work out an arrangement…"

"Good evening," the man responded abruptly. Poker-faced, he waved good-bye to Nathaniel. The innkeeper had no time for deadbeats, especially ones whom he considered rude.

"You don't understand, you see I…"

"I said goodbye. Out of my place," he interrupted.

Nathaniel could see that there was no way the innkeeper was going to listen to another word he was saying. He turned and walked out the door, the innkeeper right behind him, hands on his hips.

"Hold up," the innkeeper suddenly said.

"Yes?" Nathaniel turned and answered, hoping the innkeeper may be having a change of heart.

"Is that your mule over there?" he asked.

"Yes…"

"Then get him out of my stall!" he bellowed.

"My luck runs true," Nathaniel groused to himself.

He led Khamore from the stall and into the night, back up the dark path, the innkeeper watching his every step, making sure he was on his way.

Nathaniel wandered the dark streets having no idea where he was going or what he was going to do. The night air was beginning to hold a chill in it. He shuddered and walked on. He stopped for a moment when he thought he heard voices. All was fairly silent, except for the sounds of crickets and a dog barking in the distance. He began to move on when he heard it again, and this time it was clear, voices singing in the distance. He and Khamore walked the streets guided by the melodies, attempting to discover their source. He followed the music out of curiosity and simply because he had no other place to go.

The singing led him out past the edge of the city to a crumbling wall that had once been a building. Shadows danced on the white wall, shadows made from people gathered around a fire. It was a place for drunkards and castoffs, drifters and lunatics, the poor and homeless. All Nathaniel cared about was that there was a fire and a place where he might be able to lie down.

"Who comes this way!" a voice called to him as he neared the fire. For a moment, all was silent.

"I come in peace!" was all Nathaniel could think of to say.

Two men broke from the group, walked a few feet from the fire, and faced Nathaniel. He could not make out their faces, but one was about Nathaniel's size; the other, much larger, over six-feet tall, with very broad shoulders.

"I asked who you were, not your creed!" the smaller one of them shouted as the thirty or so individuals who were gathered at the wall broke out in laughter at the comment. "Come, man, come nearer; let us take a look at you!" the shorter man ordered.

Nathaniel was beginning to question the wisdom of his decision as he cautiously approached the two men and the fire. "My name is Nathaniel, and I'm looking for a place to spend the night."

"Have you made reservations? I don't believe we have room if you have no reservations!" the same man shot back. His audience of misfits laughed again at his humor. He continued, "Well, it is short notice, but I suppose there just may be a spot for you." The speaker began motioning with his arms for Nathaniel to join them. "Move aside, move aside, people, let the man have some fire!" the smaller man ordered as Nathaniel stepped into warmth. Nathaniel's eyes met and studied the variety of shapes and ages of the faces that stared back at him as they came into the light. They appeared to be mostly men in their twenties and thirties, but there were also older men, and a few women—one of whom looked exceptionally old and haggard. There were even a couple of children.

"Welcome, Nathaniel, to our camp. My name is Platon," he stated, holding out his hand. Somehow he looked different from the others, a step above them. He was about Nathaniel's age with thinning red hair, and he was clean-shaven. "And my friend here is Marcello," he said, putting his hand on the big man's shoulder. "We welcome strangers here, but I warn you, Marcello will make very short work of you if you are here to cause trouble!" Nathaniel glanced over at Marcello, who stood with folded arms, his big bearded face scowling back at Nathaniel.

"Don't worry, I can assure you, trouble is nothing I want right now."

"Then why do you torment me so?" Platon entreated.

"Torment you?" Nathaniel was completely puzzled.

"I see you have brought my first wife with you," he exclaimed loudly, looking at Khamore, "Oh, I'm truly sorry, on closer inspection I see this could not be her, for my first wife was fair-haired!" Laughter again followed, and even Nathaniel had to laugh as he peered into Khamore's homely face.

"Warm yourself by the fire, Nathaniel, for the Romans have not yet found a way to place a tax on its heat! We are poor, but we are not without our resources. Would you care for some pottage?" Platon asked, reaching over the fire and stirring a scorched black pot with a wooden spoon.

"Yes, thank you very much," Nathaniel answered eagerly. He was handed a crudely carved wooden bowl, filled to the top with the contents of the pot, along with a hunk of bread. The smell met his nostrils, and he trembled with anticipation, for the day's journey had left him with a ravenous hunger. He used the bread as a spoon and hungrily shoveled the stew into his mouth.

"This is delicious!" he mumbled through the food in his mouth. Manners seemed quite unimportant to him at this moment. "Would it be rude for me to ask what I am eating?" Nathaniel asked, though it tasted so good he cared very little.

"Almost anything we could find, wild vegetables and spices, roots, and this afternoon an unfortunate quail."

"Crept up on him, caught him with my bare hands, I did!" A gravely voice interjected proudly. It was Marcello.

"He does seem to have a strange gift for that sort of thing," Platon remarked with an uplifted eyebrow. "Marcello is a bit slow in the head," Platon whispered to Nathaniel, "caught the fever a few years back, never been the same. But he's as quick as a fox and as strong as an ox!"

Nathaniel filled his bowl three times before he had finally had enough. Platon was quite a talker, telling tales to the crowd as Nathaniel ate. It was soon evident that he was their undeclared leader and, judging by his vocabulary and his humor, quite intelligent. He carried a large wine sack about his neck and drank from it liberally.

"Nathaniel!" Platon shouted, slapping him on the back. "Now that you have eaten your fill, it is time to pay for your supper!"

"Pay for my supper… ? What do you mean?" he asked nervously. "I have no money!"

"No money is needed my friend! You owe us a tale, a song, maybe a story from your homeland. Where are you from?"

"Where am I from?" Nathaniel repeated uncomfortably, for he remembered Ethan's advice to say as little as possible about himself. "Well, far away. A long way from here," he answered curtly.

"Say no more, for I detect from your voice that the subject is one you do not care to talk about. Many of us here have secrets, unpleasant pasts; most of it is better left dead and buried."

"Thank you," he sighed, relieved.

"But you still owe us a story or a song."

"I don't think so, you see I don't really know any stories or songs that you'd…"

"Can you believe that," Nathaniel heard a voice in the crowd cry out. "He eats our food, and now he considers our company below him."

"It really is most impolite," remarked Platon.

"Very impolite!" growled Marcello.

Nathaniel felt all eyes on him; and it was apparent that if he didn't think of something fast, he could be finding another place to stay the night.

"All right then, let me think," Nathaniel's mind desperately tried to think of something, anything that he knew or remembered that these people from long ago would understand or find interesting. Then a poem from his youth, something he had memorized as a teenager for school came to him. But that was so long ago, could he still recall it?

"I think I might have one," he finally announced. "I will do my best to tell it to you." He closed his eyes so as not to be distracted by the stares that seemed to bore into him, and began.

"When the sky… no… that's not right. What was it now? Wait a minute, I think I remember!" he exclaimed.

> When the sun sinks to rest,
> And the star of the west
> Sheds its soft silver light over the sea,
> What sweet thoughts arise,
> As the dim twilight dies
> For then am I thinking of thee!
> Oh then crowding fast

Come the joys of the past
Through the dimness of days long gone by,
Like the stars peeping out,
Through the darkness about,
From the soft silent depth of the sky.
And thus, as the night
Grows more lovely and bright
With the clustering of planet and star,
So this darkness of mine
Wins a radiance divine
From the light that still lingers afar,
Then welcome the night
With its soft holy light!
In its silence my heart is more free
The rude world to forget,
Where no pleasure I've met,
Since the hour that I parted from thee.

Nathaniel let out a sigh of relief after he finished the last line of the poem. After his false start he was amazed that he had recalled every line without stumbling. All was silent now but for the soft hiss and crackling of the fire.

"I think that was the most beautiful thing I've ever heard!" a raspy voice said. It was Marcello, who began dabbing at his eyes with his sleeve.

"Yes, very nice, very nice indeed," Platon said quietly. He suddenly appeared quite melancholy, staring into the fire with a faraway look in his eye. "Is that something you wrote yourself?"

"Oh, no, hardly! It was written by a man… Oh, what was his name? Love… Love… Lover. That's it, Lover! I remember his name because after reading the poem, I was somewhat amused by the name of its author. I thought it was appropriate."

"Quite appropriate," Platon acknowledged. "Here's to him," he said and held up his wine sack again and took a long drink from it.

"Would you care for some wine?" he asked Nathaniel. "It is not the finest, but it does comfort the soul."

"No, thank you. I really would like to find a spot around here to rest for the night though. I have had a long day."

"Of course; pick a spot. But it seems you have no blanket, and it does get quite cold out here." He motioned to Marcello, who left and came back with a thin, heavy, wool cover.

"Take this. It will make your night more pleasant," Platon explained as Marcello handed the blanket to Nathaniel. "I had planned to make merry tonight, but your poem entered me like a cool stream and put out my fire. I will join you, if you do not object, and discuss the world with you before sleep overtakes us." The crowd moaned at his words, disappointed that Platon was retiring. Nathaniel would have preferred to decline the invitation, for his eyelids were already heavy, but he was not eager to offend someone who had been such a gracious host.

"Marcello, fetch me my blanket, and take care of Nathaniel's mule for him." Marcello returned with another blanket and then led Khamore away. With the exception of just a few of the people, all others seemed to take their cue from Platon and began laying their blankets on the ground, readying themselves for bed.

Suddenly, a loud scream penetrated the night: "The stars have eyes; and they watch us; they know our deeds! They will come to us in the night and steal our souls if we let them. Beware! Purify yourselves! Purify yourselves!" A man sprang from the crowd with madness in his eyes, and ran straight for the fire. He looked like a wild man, with long tangled hair on his head and face, and clothing that was shredded and hanging from his body in strips. He grabbed the end of a thick burning stick and was about to thrust it into his chest when two men dove on him and pushed him to the ground. Sparks flew up into the blackness as the burning wood was knocked from his hands and fell to the earth. He was only on the ground for a moment when another bloodcurdling scream came from him and the two men who had jumped on top of him were hurled backward, both narrowly missing landing in the fire. The wild man jumped to his feet again and made another dash for the fire. A large figure suddenly stepped in front of him, and with a crashing blow, sent the wild man falling to the ground unconscious.

Platon looked more irritated than upset. He glanced over at Marcello who was standing over the unconscious lunatic. "Pick him up, Marcello, and lay him back down on his blanket and cover him." He then shouted to the two men who had attempted to stop the madman, "Tie your brother up; sit on him if you have to, but don't let him get away from you again! I'll not have him annoying us tonight, I'm in no mood for it!" The two men followed Marcello who dumped the unconscious man back on his blanket.

Nathaniel stared over at the man, wide-eyed.

"Don't concern yourself with it, Nathaniel. It was a fit; that's all it was. He has them fairly often and he's more of a harm to himself than to others. Besides, I think Marcello put a good enough knock on his jaw to have him out for the night." Platon sat down near the fire and pulled his blanket around him. The outburst didn't seem to shake the others either, and they resumed their preparations for bedding down. Nathaniel tried to put the picture of the demented man about to impale himself with a burning stick out of his mind. He drew his blanket around himself and lay on the ground near the fire.

Platon stared deeply into the fire. "I will not keep you long, because I know you are tired. But it is obvious that you are educated, and tonight I am desirous of intelligent conversation."

"Thank you," replied Nathaniel, somewhat flattered.

"Nathaniel, tell me, are you a religious man? Do you believe in a god?"

The question was so direct and unexpected, that at first it startled him. "God... oh, sure I believe in God," he muttered.

"I am a philosopher, Nathaniel. Not a great one, mind you, but I ponder such things, and I am not so sure about God. That is why I am here, in Bethany, and it causes great sorrow for my friends and family. I have been away now for almost a year. Your poem caused me to yearn for them."

"What is there in Bethany for you?" Nathaniel asked. "And where, if you don't mind me asking, are you from?"

"I am a Roman," he said with a smile. "Does that surprise you? I come from a very wealthy Roman family, one with influence and power. My father is a scholar and had always been fascinated with the Greek culture, hence my name, Platon, after the Greek philosopher Plato."

"I don't want to appear skeptical, Platon but if you come from such a family, what are you doing living with… with… " Nathaniel struggled for a polite word.

"Paupers?" Platon finished his sentence for him. "I must confess I do not, nor have I ever, fit in very well with Rome's elite. I seem to have more of a kindred spirit with these people. I found Roman conversations and their conclusions empty and hollow, and I less than subtly let them know it. But even I, with such influential lineage, was subject to the penalties of Rome; and my quest for God and truth was bringing me into conflict with those in power. My questions were too daring, too bold, for some say Caesar himself is a god. If I had stayed there much longer, my life would have been forfeited, and my questions forever left unanswered. So I left Rome in search of the answer. I do not spend all my time among the poor here, but as much as I can, for I enjoy their company. I afford them much protection because of my name and because I am a Roman citizen. They are not abused when I am around."

"But Bethany? Why Bethany? What possibly could be here for you?"

"Not Bethany, Nathaniel, Jerusalem. For even in Rome we hear of its reputation, that God favors it, that it is reputed to be his jewel. I have seen the Jewish slaves in my land shrivel and die after being taken from it, like they were a plant pulled up by its roots. God must be in Jerusalem, I reasoned, for never have I seen a people respond in such a way!" he expounded excitedly, gesturing wildly with his hands.

He continued, "My concept of God had always been so impersonal. I thought that if God did exist, he was not involved in creation but was set apart from it, always trying to create order from disorder, forever trying to shape a rational form from chaotic matter. For this reason, some philosophers have even gone so far as to say that God is forever doing geometry," he commented, stopping to laugh. "But I saw something different in those people, the ones called Jews. They seemed to live and breathe their God."

"But why then are you in Bethany?" Nathaniel wondered aloud.

Plato chuckled, "Because of that man. That teacher."

"What teacher? Who do you mean?"

"The one they call Jesus. I followed him here. I became aware of him almost as soon as I arrived in Jerusalem. My father is related to a woman there, the wife of a procurator. I asked about Jesus shortly after my arrival, and I remember her saying, 'Stay away from that one, Platon. I have had nightmares about that man, he troubles me greatly,'" Platon cackled, shaking his finger in the air as he mimicked her voice. "Sometimes I wish I had listened to her."

"Why do you say that?"

"I follow him from afar, from a distance. The first time I heard him, I was one of hundreds sitting on the side of a hill. His words cut through me like a knife, and all my learning, my logic, was useless. It blew away like feathers in the wind! For he spoke to my heart, not my mind! I came to Jerusalem to find God; and I end up sitting at the feet of a poor carpenter, who reveals more truth and wisdom to me about God than all the great teachers from Rome or Greece!"

Nathaniel was taken aback, for while Platon's words described tribute, his voice resonated with frustration. Platon paused and took another drink from his wine sack.

"You seem upset, Platon. I don't understand. It sounds like you have found what you were looking for."

"That's the problem. I... don't know. I don't know if I am capable of doing the things that he says men ought to do. He speaks of casting away your worldly goods and denying the lust of the flesh and following him. If I were capable of doing those things, what good would it do? For it would only mean death if I ever ventured back to Rome and espoused it. But every time I think that I can leave and forget him, I hear his voice calling me, and I am drawn back. I return again, a face in the back of the crowd, never able to leave and yet not able to remain, forever in between, perpetually in torment! What a fool I was to come here. I think I am worse off than when I started." Platon stared wide-eyed into the fire for a moment, a look of anguish on his face. He quickly shook it off, and, a little embarrassed, turned to Nathaniel.

"I'm sorry to carry on like that—it must be this wine talking!" he quickly exclaimed, but took another drink from it anyway. "Enough about that!" he exclaimed, slapping his knees with both hands and injecting a decidedly more positive tone in his voice.

"Let us discuss truth, and how one finds it. It is said that a man cannot inquire about that which he knows, or about that which he does not know; for if he knows, he has no need to inquire; and if not, he cannot; for he does not know the subject about which he is to inquire. Do you agree with that or conversely..." A snore coming from Nathaniel interrupted Platon in midsentence.

Platon laughed, "I guess that is your answer, and I can't say that I totally disagree! I envy you Nathaniel, for two men wage a mortal war within my head and allow me no rest. Sleep well, my friend, sleep well."

CHAPTER TWELVE

Sing a Song of Death

Nathaniel was not sure what it was that woke him from his deep sleep. It might have been that he was not accustomed to sleeping on the hard, cold ground, or it could have been the odd murmuring voices that seemed to creep into his sleep. But whatever it was, he awoke with a start and found himself staring wide-eyed into the fire. He could not have been asleep long, he reasoned, for the fire was not much lower than when he had dozed off. He felt uneasy, and a sense of dread seemed to be engulfing him. His eyes moved around the camp, but everything seemed to be as it should. He could hear no murmuring voices, only the heavy breathing of those asleep and the popping and crackling of the fire. He attributed his apprehension to his unusual supper. "Crept up on him, caught him with my bare hands, I did." Nathaniel smiled as he remembered Marcello's raspy voice bragging how he had caught the quail. Satisfied that all was well, Nathaniel's eyes began to close again, taking one last glance in the direction of Platon, who was a couple of feet from him. Nathaniel let out a gasp and stiffened in horror.

Platon was still awake, sitting there with his blanket wrapped around him, gazing deep into the flames of the fire. But squatting on either side of him were two dreadful-looking creatures, similar in size and appearance to the demon that he had seen with Mullyrug when he was on the road to Bethany.

Nathaniel shut his eyes and shivered. Could it be just a bad dream? That would not be surprising considering how unusual the last day had been. Fear and horror began to swallow him, and he squeezed his eyes shut and tried to forget what he had thought that he had seen. But then he heard the strange voices.

"To live is useless, useless; come for the sweetness, the sweetness," a sickeningly sweet, sing-song voice softly hissed. "Death is sweet, a rest for the weary; all will be well then, yes, death is the answer; taste its goodness!"

Another voice soon entered, whose inflections and vocabulary were very articulate. His words cut like a knife, with cunning and slyness as its edge. "Consider, Platon, your situation. You are nothing but a fail-ure, a coward, an over-educated sot. You are nothing like your family; they are proud and noble Romans all. You, seeking after truth. Ha! You know the truth, don't you? You are an undisciplined drunk who follows phantoms and illusions because reality causes you too much pain. You hide behind your noble journeys, your quest for truth and God. Look at you, a drunken fool and a coward! Be brave Platon—end your shame, embrace death like a man. You are a Roman!"

Nathaniel could take it no longer, so he slowly opened his eyes again. Platon was still sitting there motionless, staring, almost as if he were in a trance. The two strange creatures were standing now, walking slowly around him, one softly singing, the other continuing in its tireless diatribe. Platon seemed totally unaware of his company, for his eyes followed none of their movements nor did he respond to any of their accusations. His only movement was to bring the wine sack to his lips and then bring it back down again. Nathaniel then remembered Ethan's words to him, "Let your eyes see clearly the things that are unseen." Now he understood. His eyes had been opened to the supernatural.

"Dear Jesus," he whispered, almost inaudibly. Almost inaudibly. For as those words left his mouth, the two creatures stopped dead in their tracks, and a shiver could be seen going through both of them.

"Who said that? Did you hear that, Telute?" the articulate one said.

"The name, the terrible name was said, Shagah. Torment and pain, torment and pain," Telute sang back. The two figures turned and looked in

Nathaniel's direction. Nathaniel had immediately realized what had happened and feigned sleep. Telute and Shagah came and stood over him.

"This is the one; he is the one. The one who said it," sang Telute, "but he slumbers." Nathaniel was terrified, but tried to keep his breathing slow and steady, as if he were in a deep sleep.

"Possibly," replied Shagah, bending down, his ugly face almost touching Nathaniel's as he scrutinized the human, "but I sense fear coming from him. We don't want any interruptions, for I believe Platon is almost ready."

"Perhaps a dream has come to him, has come, a wonderful nightmare. It causes him to tremble and quake, to tremble and quake!"

"Perhaps, Telute. The name could have been uttered in sleep. The name is certainly no secret around here."

"Yes, no secret, no secret indeed!" The weepy voice sang. "But we must get back, to our deed, our work. I will sing a sweet song of death to him. He will listen, listen and die."

"You will sing, Telute, but it is my deception that will snare him. This one is mine, and I will demand the credit!" growled Shagah.

"We shall see; yes, we will, we shall see who the real master is, the master of death," sang back Telute. The pair moved back over to Platon and began again.

Nathaniel opened his eyes to just a slit, but he could see Platon and the two demons clearly. They both had the same serpentine look to their faces, with just a scattering of black hair on their heads. They stood about three feet tall and were naked, with bumpy, reddish-pink skin. They cast no shadow as they moved about. Their arms were long and thin, and their hands had long bony fingers that began moving up and down Platon's body, almost as if they were searching for something.

Nathaniel tried to focus his eyes, for he seemed almost to be seeing double. He could now see there was an aura around Platon, a shell or an outline of some kind that followed the shape of his body. It had a grayness to it, and the two demons moved their bony fingers all over it as they worked on him.

"He is not dark enough, not nearly dark enough," remarked Shagah. "Not like our friend over there," he snickered, a gruesome smile upon his face, looking and pointing a long bony finger in the direction of the man who had earlier tried to burn himself with fire.

"His sin is dark, dirty and dark, so in and out we go, in and out we go!" Telute sang happily as he danced toward the sleeping madman. It was difficult for Nathaniel to see all of it, but the demon Telute began running his fingers over the dark black aura of the man, almost as if he were playing a piano.

He suddenly sang out, "There it is, the right spot, the beautiful darkness," and in the blink of an eye he dove into it and disappeared into the man. The man gave a little jerk as the demon entered, but continued to sleep.

"Come out of him, we have work to do!" hissed Shagah. "Besides, you know it is more enjoyable to torment these detestable creatures when they're awake!"

Telute then popped out of the man as easily as he had entered and went back over to Platon.

Shagah cursed. "See, this one is falling asleep, I fear we have missed our chance! We must work quick if we are to have any opportunity at all tonight."

"We must stir him up, shiver and shake him, distress and vex him," added Telute. So they began again, Telute with his songs of death, Shagah with his lies and deceit; and soon Platon's face showed distress once more.

"I am worthless, I cannot go on," Platon whispered under his breath.

"Yes, you are worthless, Platon," echoed Shagah.

"Death waits; come to it; embrace it," sang Telute.

Nathaniel seemed frozen by the horror of it all, not really knowing what to do, trying to keep the fear and revulsion of the sight before him from overwhelming him.

"You are not even a Jew, Platon. The one you want to follow, the carpenter, would have nothing to do with you! It is hopeless, Platon!" Shagah hissed.

"There is no God, Platon, none at all; forsake the pain, the pain of life. Death is calling, calling. All will soon be well… " purred Telute. Platon bent his head down and put his face into his hands.

"I think we have him, Telute," Shagah smirked. "I will keep him busy. Call the others." Telute went over to the demon-possessed man, and one by one nine others came out of him.

"That is enough, the rest of you stay in him," ordered Shagah. They were dreadfully wicked, ugly, things. They all gathered around Platon and began to sing and chant.

Platon slowly lifted his head. He had a great sadness on his face as if he were resigned to his fate. He lifted his wine sack up to his mouth one more time and took a long drink. He reached inside his robe and produced a long, shiny, silver knife. He grasped the knife with both hands and turned the blade toward himself. He extended his arms out, and with tears pouring down his face prepared to plunge the blade into his chest. The demons sang and danced, whipping themselves into a frenzy.

"I cannot not lie here and do nothing!" Nathaniel thought, his anger overcoming his fear. He started to get up and was about to dive towards Platon, but it was too late.

In a blur, a figure seemed to come out of nowhere, running directly through the demons as though they were ghosts and kicked the blade from Platon's hands. The blade flew into the air and into the fire. Shagah and Telute threw themselves on to the ground and began to kick, scream, curse, and throw an unholy tantrum. The other nine dove back into the possessed man's body.

Nathaniel looked back at Platon and noticed the aura was beginning to fade around him, as were the images of Telute and Shagah. Apparently, Nathaniel's gift of spiritual eyes was only a temporary one.

Nathaniel was surprised that no one had been awakened by all the ruckus, until it dawned on him that the only sound anyone else would have heard would have been the sound of the knife landing in the fire.

"Marcello, I owe you my thanks, again… I suppose," Platon said.

"Why do you do this, Platon?" Marcello beseeched in his gravelly voice. "Every night I watch you, I make sure you go to sleep before I do, because I know, sometimes you want to plunge a knife into your chest! You are so smart, so much smarter than me! Why do you do such things, Platon?"

"I don't know, my friend… I really don't know."

Marcello's loud, raspy voice started to cause some in the camp to stir. "Is there anything wrong, Platon?" A voice called out.

"No, nothing wrong, nothing wrong at all. Marcello had a bad dream and I had to fetch some warm milk and rock him back to sleep!" Marcello shook his head back and forth with a smile on his face as a few chortles escaped from those who had awakened. "Go to sleep, go back to sleep everyone," Marcello's voice bellowed. Platon lay down and Marcello covered him with a blanket. With all the wine he had consumed, it was not long before Platon was fast asleep.

Nathaniel watched silently as Marcello then lay down himself. Nathaniel lay there for awhile, thinking. He could have arisen and tried to talk to Platon himself, he supposed, but what would he have said? That he saw demons dancing about him? No, he thought, Platon was drunk as it was, so anything Nathaniel could have told him would make more sense tomorrow.

Nathaniel was still shaken by the sights that he had seen, and ordinarily could not have slept the rest of the night. But his weariness proved stronger than his fear this evening, so it was not long before he joined the rest of the camp in slumber.

"Wake up, wake up! Come now, wake up!" an old woman's gruff voice shouted.

Nathaniel mumbled back an absurd statement from some nonsensical dream he was having.

"What are you talking about?" The woman asked incredulously, scratching the whiskers on her chin. "What foolishness is this? Get up, I say, you can not sleep here all day!" she barked and began to prod him in the side with her walking stick.

"What… what… where am… who are you?" Nathaniel groggily asked, blinking his eyes as they opened to the bright sunlight. He rubbed his hands over his face and felt the stubble of his growing beard.

"I am not your mother; that's all you need to know. Now get yourself up," she snapped.

Nathaniel sat up and looked around him. All he saw was the old woman, a few red coals and smoke coming from last night's fire. "Where is everyone? Where did everybody go?"

"Where did everybody go?" the old women repeated with her hands on her hips. "It's already into the fifth hour of the day! Do you expect people to wait until you decide to rise so that they can start their day? Hah! Laziness is probably the reason that you ended up here in the first place! It is Friday, and I wonder how many times this week that you've put in a good day's work!"

Nathaniel groaned. He was barely awake. Platon and Marcello, the only people whom he knew, had left; and now some crabby, white-haired old hag was standing over him lecturing him on his work ethic.

"Well then, tell me; Platon and Marcello—how long ago did they leave? Where did they go?"

"They left hours ago and I don't know where they went!" she barked back. "They tried to wake you but you would have none of it."

For a moment Nathaniel sat there in a daze, wondering what to do next. "Jerusalem!" he suddenly shouted. "I almost forgot. That's the reason I'm here! I've got to go to Jerusalem!" he proclaimed as he jumped to his feet. "Old woman, what is the best way to Jerusalem?"

She scrunched up her wrinkled face, "Jerusalem is only two miles from here and you don't know the way there? You take the footpath, of course, from the west side of Bethany. Everybody knows that!"

"Thank you," he said as he stretched and raised his arms to the sky in an attempt to loosen up his stiff back and legs "I really must be moving on."

"Well… I suppose you shouldn't be leaving hungry," she said walking over to a sack. "Here are some bread and figs left from this morning."

"Thank you again; that was very kind of you," he replied, surprised by her gesture.

"You better get going," she grumbled back, but Nathaniel saw a trace of a toothless grin come to her face. He walked outside of the camp to the place where Khamore was tethered to a dead tree. Nathaniel untied Khamore and stiffly got on his back.

"Good-bye, old woman!" he shouted as he trotted off. The old woman just shook her head and grimaced.

Nathaniel was soon at the edge of the city of Bethany, traveling down the footpath towards Jerusalem. He could barely contain his excitement, for he was certain that Jesus would be there at this time. After all, Ethan had set this up, so this must be his chance. He was actually going to hear a sermon from Jesus Christ. Imagine that! And who knew? Maybe if he could make his way through the crowd he could talk to Jesus himself. While Ethan had never made any such promises about seeing Jesus, much less speaking to him, Nathaniel felt assured of it. "Why else would he have brought me here at this time," he reasoned, chuckling almost giddily to himself. "Things aren't turning out so bad after all!"

Nathaniel made a clicking noise with his tongue and gently prodded Khamore with his heels. "Let's get going, Khamore. I'm anxious to get to Jerusalem!" Khamore grunted his disapproval and continued at his own pace.

Nathaniel felt the warm sun on the back of his neck. He turned and looked at the sun in the cloudless sky. Judging from its position, it appeared to be late morning.

He was beginning to notice the trees and how green everything looked in contrast to his trip through the desert, when everything around him seemed to slowly grow a bit darker. He rode on a few more feet as it grew darker still. "That's odd. There wasn't a cloud in the sky only a moment ago," he remarked as he turned to see what was obstructing the sun.

"What in the world…!" shouted Nathaniel for what he saw made his mouth drop wide open. Where the bright yellow sun had been only moments before, a large dark ball now hung in the sky. "What's happened… what's going on here?" Nathaniel nervously asked out loud as it began to grow increasingly darker.

Khamore immediately sensed the strangeness of it all, along with Nathaniel's uneasiness. He soon became irritable and began to bray and bawl. He refused to move forward and began kicking out his hind legs. Nathaniel, being the inexperienced rider that he was, was thrown from the mule almost immediately, landing with a thud on the side of the path, fortunately unhurt. "Whoa, Khamore, whoa!" he shouted as he got back on his feet and tried to calm the animal. But Khamore was spooked and suddenly took off like a shot on the path back toward Bethany.

"Come back, come back here!" Nathaniel shouted as he ran a few steps in that direction. But it was pointless to chase after the animal, for Khamore was moving uncharacteristically fast and soon disappeared into the strange grayness. Nathaniel sighed and looked back into the sky. The black ball that had been the sun still hung there, and the land was filled with an eerie dusk. Everything around him suddenly seemed to be drained of color, but at least the curious darkness allowed enough light to continue down the footpath toward Jerusalem.

Nathaniel estimated that he could be no more than a mile away from Jerusalem. He broke into a trot, anxious to end his journey, and to flee from this strange gloom. As he followed the winding path, he began to descend into what appeared to be a valley. It was then that he slowed to a stop, for a gust of wind carried to him the sound of moaning and crying of a great number of people ahead.

Nathaniel stood stone still. His heart was racing not only from running, but also from fear. Fear of the strange gloom that wanted to swallow him, and now the weeping and wailing that accompanied it. Ethan had told him to go to Jerusalem, but how could he go on not knowing what awaited him just ahead? He stood almost paralyzed with indecision and confusion; for if he turned and went back the other way, where would he go? Certainly nothing was back there for him. His mind was spinning in circles when he made out two dark figures coming toward him. He ran a few yards from the path and lay flat on the ground in some brush and watched.

The two dark figures said nothing as they neared the spot where he had been standing. Then one of them spoke and Nathaniel immediately jumped to his feet. For that deep, raspy, voice he heard was so distinctive it could only belong to one man: Marcello!

"Marcello!" he shouted and ran forward. As he drew nearer he recognized the other figure as Platon. "Platon, am I ever glad to see you!

What is going on around here?" Nathaniel felt comforted by just seeing their familiar faces.

Platon and Marcello eyed him warily. "Do we know you, sir?" Platon questioned. "I warn you, I am in no mood for folly, and if this be some sort of trick or trap—if robbery is your motive, I will advise you, we are Roman citizens!" he charged.

"Platon, it's me, Nathaniel! Remember, I stopped at your camp last night!"

Marcello interceded. "Platon, he was the man with the ugly mule."

Platon stared at Nathaniel for a moment and then recognition came to his face. "Nathaniel, oh yes," he muttered, smiling only slightly. "Please forgive me, but I drank far too much wine last night and today I have other things on my mind."

"Tell me, Platon, what is this darkness about and all the weeping and moaning that I hear?"

"This darkness… I can't explain it. I have never seen the likes of this, nor have the peasants that dwell in the Kidron Valley behind me. They weep and moan and beat their breasts, for they fear it is the end of the world; for all that I know, they may be right. Can anyone doubt that a hand has reached out and grabbed the sun? I tremble greatly too, for I am abashed to think that it is my brethren who may be the cause of this calamity!"

"Your brethren… what are you talking about? What could they possibly have to do with this?"

"Rome… Romans… their military, their politicians! They crush anything that they do not understand! Death and violence have become my people's meat, their sustenance!" Platon screamed with rage into the heavens, his fists in the air. "But now, I fear, they have eaten a bitter herb, one that may bring death to them and all others!" He sank to his knees and fell sobbing onto the ground.

Nathaniel was shaken by Platon's conduct, but still had no idea what Platon was trying to tell him. Finally Marcello spoke solemnly, "That carpenter, Jesus. The one we have been following, the one they say is the Son of God. They are crucifying him as we speak."

CHAPTER THIRTEEN

The Ultimate Battle

"**N**athaniel, where are you going?" Marcello asked.

"I was sent to Jerusalem, Marcello, and I must go there," Nathaniel explained grimly as he made his way past the two men.

"Why? Why don't you come with us, for who knows what awaits those in Jerusalem!" Platon said weepily, lifting his head from his hands.

"I think I know," was all Nathaniel said as he walked away down the path into the darkness. He made his way into the Kidron Valley and passed through a weeping, terrified crowd. "Which way to Golgotha?" he asked a stranger.

"Go straight ahead to the gates of the city, and then follow the road north. Follow the road around the walls of the city. It will lead you there." It was not a long walk, and Nathaniel soon reached the northern end of the city. He rounded the corner and then followed the road as it curved south. It was then that he could see its shape through the dark, gloomy gray. There it was, between the road he stood on and the walls of Jerusalem. That horrible hill. The hill of pain and sorrow, the hill of death. Golgotha.

Step by step he went, and with each step the darkness gave way; and the hill began to become clearer, as did the three wooden crosses atop it. A small crowd had gathered near its base. A few jeered and shouted accusations, some just stood and stared. Others wept softly. A small group of soldiers sat on top of the hill a few yards from the crucifixions.

Nathaniel stepped off the road and made his way closer. When he was about thirty feet from the crowd, he stopped and leaned against a nearby tree. Lightening began streaking across the dark but cloudless sky, and thunder soon followed. He turned and faced the tree, burying his face in his arms. He did not want to go any farther. He began to tremble, suddenly realizing how unworthy he really was to be here. Who was he to stand on this ground, to intrude on this sacred event? He was close enough now to be able to see the faces of those on the cross, but he could not lift up his eyes to bear the sight.

"I am not worthy to be here, for I am a sinful man!" he cried, weeping into his arms. "I am afraid; forgive me!" he prayed. Nathaniel leaned against the tree and wept for some time, until he began to hear the sound of voices in his ears, voices that seemed to be growing steadily louder and increasing in number. He pulled himself together and wiped the tears from his face with the sleeve from his robe. He lifted up his head and looked around him.

His eyes grew wide, and he grasped his head in his hands and muttered, "Oh no… no!"

For Nathaniel's spiritual eyes were opened once more; and hundreds, no, thousands of demons suddenly began to take form around him. Out of nowhere they came—in front of him, behind him, to the side of him; they seemed to be everywhere. Nathaniel let out a cry of shock and repulsion; and in a fit of panic, frantically made his way fifteen feet up the tree and straddled a large branch. The demons took no notice of him at all, for they were there for one purpose and one purpose only.

> We've snatched the one, who claims to be king,
> We've used the lash, we've heard it sing
> And now we have him, nailed to a tree!
> Death to the king of kings! Yeah!
> Death to the king of kings!

Hundreds of demons chanted this horrible rhyme over and over beneath him. Nathaniel squeezed his eyes shut and covered his head with his hands, but it was no use, for he could not stop the demonic chorus from offending his ears. He drew up enough courage to look around him once again. What his eyes took in astonished him even the more.

As impossible as it might seem, there were now even more demons than before. They were vile, repulsive-looking things, with faces and bodies only found in nightmares. Some resembled Platon's tormentors, Shagah and Telute; others were closer in shape to Mullyrug. Some were almost beyond description, so grotesque and hideous in appearance that they made Nathaniel feel more nauseated than frightened. Hordes and hordes of them began gathering around the hill of Golgotha and the three crosses suspended in it. Then, for the first time, Nathaniel let his eyes go up the hill to the cross in the middle, the one that held Jesus.

Even through the grayness, he could see the terrible wounds that covered Jesus' body. His torso was covered with welts and stripes, so much so that the wood below his feet was completely red from his flowing blood. Red covered the ground beneath the cross. Nathaniel's eyes slowly and sadly made their way up to the face of Jesus. Nathaniel groaned and turned away, for it was hard for him to bear such a sight. How could one human have done such a thing to another! Jesus' eyes were almost swollen shut from the games the soldiers had played with him the night before, for they had blindfolded him and struck him and mocked him asking, "Prophesy, who is it that hit you?" His nose and cheekbones were also swollen, and the crown of thorns that they had planted on his head produced a steady stream of blood that ran down his face.

Nathaniel's eyes found their way back to the cross, and then to the two men crucified on each side of Christ. Soon he noticed something else, something he had also seen the night before. Both men had a dirty gray aura around their bodies, just like Platon's. "Dark, dark with sin!" he recalled one of the demon's saying. His eyes moved back to Christ, who also had an aura about him, yet his was crystal clear!

As Nathaniel looked about, the walls of the city of Jerusalem behind the crosses seemed to be fading away. In fact, everything of this world seemed to be growing dim, save the three crosses on the hill. As the objects of this world faded and disappeared, images from the other world began to take form and shape. Images of angels, hundreds of thousands of white-robed angels, as far as Nathaniel could see, encircled the demonic horde. Mighty and powerful angels, some with flaming swords and others sitting upon great horses, all standing perfectly still, appearing like great white marble statues, each with the same terrible look of sorrow and despair on their faces.

Nathaniel's heart leapt. "Destroy them, drive the demons away!" he beckoned to them.

"It is forbidden," he heard a voice answer from inside his head.

The demons soon sensed that they had free reign and grew increasingly bold. The noise from their incessant chanting, wailing, and screaming increased. They began inching their way up the hill, up Golgotha, drawing closer, taunting, and hurling blasphemies and abominations.

"You are not the Christ! You are an imposter! If you are the Christ, save yourself! Prove it to us. Come down off the cross!" they shrieked and snickered.

"If you are the Christ, save thyself and us," echoed one of the men crucified next to him.

"You have died for nothing, no one will remember you, or what you have done! You have failed! You have failed!" hissed the demons. The scene before Nathaniel's eyes seemed to go on forever.

Nathaniel moaned to himself, "Stop it; someone please stop this." But just when he thought that things could become no worse, something even more dreadful began to happen. From everywhere and out of nowhere, wisps of darkness appeared, joining together in a sinister cloud and started moving toward the cross that held Jesus. Even the demonic forces were at first stunned by its appearance, not knowing what to make of it, and a hush fell upon them.

Then, one screamed with delight, "It is sin! It is sin! It has come for even him!" A great cheer rang out among them.

Like a thousand dark asps the wisps came, floating and gliding silently and threateningly toward their destination. Closer and closer they advanced, until one landed upon him, upon the only man who had never known sin. Jesus let out a low moan. Then another came upon him and another, and soon they were all about him. But still more came, bringing with them their feelings of guilt and shame. They soon began to cover his aura, until all Nathaniel could see was his battered and bruised face. The demons worked themselves into a frenzy at the sight, dancing and singing, cursing and hissing at him.

"Behold, the lamb of God, that taketh away the sins of the world!" Nathaniel tearfully whispered.

Suddenly a roar came up from the demonic camp. "Make way! Make way! Make way for the ruler and the true king of earth!" A growling demonic voice exclaimed.

Nathaniel looked behind him and saw the demonic crowd part. They all fell on their faces, throwing their long thin arms in front of them and became stone silent. Then, in the distance, he saw an awesome sight. A man… an angel… someone was coming. The being was clad in a great billowing robe and cape, made of such wondrous colors, colors so bright and bold they were beyond description or earthly imagination. He came forward, appearing to glide over the ground. His face was handsome beyond any mortal looks and light seemed to emanate from it. A soft wind flowed through his golden hair as he moved forward. He soon passed under the tree were Nathaniel sat and made his way towards the cross.

"Hail, Lucifer!" a growling voice exclaimed to the crowd.

"Hail, Lucifer!" a deafening answer reverberated back, exploding from the demonic crowd. Again and again they shouted it until Nathaniel thought he would go mad. Finally, with his back to them and facing Golgotha, their ruler raised his arms, and just as quickly the demons became silent. He slowly turned toward them, his arms still raised, and spoke. "Victory! Victory! Victory is ours!" he dramatically exclaimed. And with that, the roar of "Hail, Lucifer!" again returned.

"Some have proclaimed and prophesied," he began, the horde falling immediately silent at the sound of his voice, "that I would bruise his heel, while he would bruise my head. I ask you, my dear followers, does it appear that I may have bruised more than his heel?" He asked this question coyly, and then grandly gestured toward the cross. The demons jumped to their feet in adulation, and began their chant again. Lucifer raised his arms and all became quiet again. He turned and looked at Jesus.

"Look at you! Just look at you! I know you can see me. Do you remember what I had offered you? I offered you all the kingdoms of the world, but you refused! Would you like me to offer it to you again?" he mocked and began to laugh. "I imagine you would. You claimed to be the Son of God, come to mend the relationship between God and man! I am puzzled though. How will you do it up there, nailed on a cross, oh Son of God?" he challenged, with feigning concern. "I am aghast! Did your beloved humans do this to you? You offered them your love, so many years ago in the garden... Do you remember? But they listened to me then, just as they have listened to me now. They've always belonged to me, surely you must know that by now! But I must confess, if I had my way, I would nail all of them to a tree also!" he boasted, laughing maniacally. "Oh what a grand time that would be! Perhaps someday... "

He gazed at the cross, shaking his head back and forth. "Look at you! Oh no... could it be?" he asked in feigned amazement. "There is sin, sin all over you. Now I know you cannot be the Messiah!"

The physical pain from the beatings and the crucifixion screamed through every fiber in Jesus' body. Beyond that, he now carried the weight and shame of a world of sin on his shoulders, sin that separated himself from God. He raised his head toward heaven and cried out as a man, "My God, my God, why hast thou forsaken me?"

Lucifer raised his arms in victory at those words, and another horrible cheer arose from his grisly minions. "You heard him! He is God forsaken, he is Godforsaken!" he screamed.

But at that same moment, something remarkable happened. The darkness, the sins of the world that had all but swallowed Jesus, slowly began to flow off of him, carried away down to the foot of the cross with his blood. There it dissolved into nothingness, and his aura could be seen once more. Clean and clear. Nathaniel stared, spellbound by the sight. A small smile grew into a joyous grin, and he suddenly remembered an old hymn. He began to sing it softly to himself:

I see a crimson stream of blood,
it flows from Calvary,
Its waves, which reach the throne of God,
are sweeping over me.

"What is this? What is this?" Lucifer questioned nervously as he watched the sin dissolve away before his eyes. But before he could even answer the question himself, Jesus' cried out loud and strong, "It is finished!"

For a moment there was total silence and time seemed to freeze. Then a lone demonic voice cried out "We have won! Hail, Lucifer, master and true king of earth!" The words were met with a deafening roar. "Hail, Lucifer! Hail, Lucifer!" They shouted over and over again.

Another deafening roar of "Hail, Lucifer" was just erupting when it happened: At that moment, the fullness of God that resided in Jesus Christ burst forth from his body. It exploded from him, with a white, holy light, pure and divine! Suddenly, shrieks of agony and terror now came from the demonic camp.

But that was only the beginning. For the light grew whiter and whiter, like a thousand suns. The demons threw themselves violently on the ground, covering their faces, shrieking and screaming. Nathaniel could hear them as they cried out, "Mercy! Have mercy upon us! Do not torment us before our time! You alone are Lord; you alone are Lord!"

Lucifer's grand clothes and physical appearance were consumed by the light, and he too appeared as the rest of them, a despicable, reptilian-like creature. He fell to the ground also and begged for mercy.

The light consumed Nathaniel on his perch in the tree. Because of its searing whiteness, he too had to turn and hide his face from it. He felt it sweep over him and engulf him, and he trembled and marveled at the power of the Almighty God. The wailing from the demons grew louder and louder in Nathaniel's ears as they rolled upon the ground and convulsed. He could hear their pathetic groveling and begging coming from the ground below him.

"Send us away from this place, oh Holy One! We cannot bear the light, the light from the Perfect One. We are the wretched, an abomination to all that is good! Have mercy on us, let us back into the darkness!"

Then the voices began to slowly fade from his ears until they were gone. He squinted out of one eye and looked down to the ground, seeing nothing but grass. As he examined the things around him, the walls of the city of Jerusalem had returned, and everything was again as it should be, for his spiritual eyes had left him. With shaking hands, Nathaniel carefully climbed down to the base of the tree. He looked past what was left of the crowd of mourners and mockers to the cross of Jesus and began to pray. But before he had said much of his prayer, he suddenly felt the ground shift beneath his feet. Rocks and boulders around the countryside began to split and burst, as the earth responded to the spirit of the Almighty God being loosed from its fleshly shell. Men and woman began to scream and run everywhere. Nathaniel saw a guard come tumbling down Golgotha's hill and heard another exclaim, "Surely, this man was the Son of God!" Graves burst open and the dead arose, so strong was God's spirit upon the land.

The ground began to open beneath Nathaniel's feet, and he lunged and somersaulted forward. He jumped to his feet and ran for the road, where he was almost run over by a man trying to control his panicked horse. The street suddenly began to come alive with people and animals fleeing in alarm.

"Watch out!" he heard a voice shout. He turned in response just as the wheels of a horse-drawn cart flew by him, grazing his shoulder and knocking him hard to the ground. The world began to spin, and then all was dark.

"Ethan, Ethan, where am I? Am I dead?"

Ethan smiled, "Are you dead? You asked me that once before as I sat by the fire; and again I will give you the same answer as I did before. You are not dead."

"Then where are we? Where could we be?" Nathaniel questioned.

"You are somewhere between life and death. A safe place, a place where we can talk before you return."

Nathaniel felt so light, so peaceful as he looked about him. He seemed to be walking in a cloud, and hues representing every color of the rainbow danced about him everywhere. Nathaniel stopped, "What if I don't want to go back? What if I wanted to stay here with you?"

"I would have to say that that is quite impossible. I do not belong here, and neither do you. This is not a destination. Besides, your life is not over yet, not by a long way."

Nathaniel understood. He began to walk again, and as he did, he began to ponder the miraculous things that he had seen and all that had happened to him.

"What are you thinking, Nathaniel?"

"I was thinking about the cross, about how all seemed lost there, how sin and Lucifer's army appeared to have won a great victory, and how there looked to be no way out. Then suddenly everything changed! Sin could not stand in the way of Jesus, neither could Satan, his deceptions, or all the demons from hell! They were absolutely no match for the spirit of the Almighty God. In fact, they were powerless before it! You should have seen what happened, Ethan!"

"I did," Ethan answered quietly.

"Oh… yes…. I'm sorry, Ethan. I forgot," Nathaniel said somewhat sheepishly.

"You're only human," he replied with a smile. "Go on, Nathaniel."

"Well, I was saying, the spirit of God is just so remarkable! It was so pure and white, so strong; yet I felt the most incredible sense of love surround me as it enveloped me! And the effect it had on evil! The demons fell to the ground, defenseless, begging to escape it!

"That moment was seared into their being for all eternity," Ethan added. "It is something they will never forget."

"Can you imagine what humans could do if God ever made such a power available to them?" Nathaniel exclaimed

"You have the power, Nathaniel. You know that."

"What do you mean, Ethan? How can I have such power?"

"Pray, Nathaniel. Pray and remember," Ethan repeated and began to walk away. Nathaniel tried to follow but found something holding him back. He struggled against it, but his struggle was in vain as he felt himself being pulled downward through the clouds and lights.

"Wait, Ethan, wait for me! There is so much more I need to ask you! Don't leave me!"

Ethan was gone, but his words echoed everywhere:

"Pray and remember; pray and remember."

CHAPTER FOURTEEN

Unfinished Business

"**W**ait, Ethan, come back; there is so much more... so much more... I need... I need..." Nathaniel heard himself mutter. His eyes fluttered, and then opened. It was daylight. He looked around and found himself lying on the ground at the bottom of a large pile of leaves. His robe and sandals were gone, replaced by his tennis shoes and jacket. He pushed himself up and rose to his feet, taking in all of his surroundings.

"I'm back... I'm home..." he whispered in amazement as his eyes took in the piles of compost about him. A smile began to creep across his face.

"I'm home!" Nathaniel shouted. "I made it! Thank you, God!" he exclaimed loudly, jumping and raising his arms into the air. He again looked around him, and everything was as it should be; no sand, no sea, just the trees and compost piles. He could even hear the noise of the traffic coming from Highway 61. He began to take a few steps toward the dirt road when he thought he heard a voice say, "Pray and remember; pray and remember."

"Ethan, is that you?" he asked. He turned, but no one was there.

"Pray and remember; pray and remember," echoed in his mind. Nathaniel turned and took a few steps back. He paused and thought for a moment, then knelt down into the pile of leaves, making it a crude alter, and began to pray. As he prayed, his thoughts went to the cross and what he had witnessed. He recalled all the demons of hell before him, how they frightened and overwhelmed him, and how he had believed that they were in complete control of the situation. It had been hopeless, he had thought, and it appeared that Christ himself had been defeated. Then the sin that encompassed him, which he had taken upon himself, fell from him and was destroyed. Nathaniel remembered back to when the spirit of God was released from the body of Christ, how the searing white holy light that came forth sent the powers of darkness reeling. The spirit tormented and disabled them, and they convulsed and begged for the darkness. "That moment is seared into their being for all eternity," he recalled Ethan telling him.

"Pray and remember; pray and remember." Once more those words echoed through his mind. Nathaniel began to pray more earnestly, and again he remembered the white holy light. This time, however, he recalled how it had surrounded and enveloped him, and how he had felt not only God's tremendous power, but also his love. It was a warm feeling, a feeling that brought him back to the first time he had come to church. Back to the first time he felt God's spirit talk to him.

"You have the power, Nathaniel, you know that," Ethan had said.

He raised his arms to the heavens, and he felt the spirit of God come upon him as when he first believed. It went deep inside him and seemed to surge through him and around him, healing and strengthening him. Nathaniel felt its goodness and holiness sweep over him, purifying and restoring his spirit. Soon it began to well up within him and begin to flow through him like a mighty river. He rose to his feet, and out of his mouth came the springs of living water.

"You have been too far away from me, my son. I have missed you," he felt the spirit of God say to him. Tears began to freely roll down Nathaniel's cheeks.

"I'm sorry, Lord; forgive me. I have missed you too," Nathaniel's spirit groaned. And so he prayed and communed with God among the dead and rotting piles of leaves.

Nathaniel did not know how long he was there before he finally felt ready to leave, for time and the measure of it seemed irrelevant at the moment. He felt brand new, confident, euphoric, to everything seemed so clear to him now: who God was, and his purpose for his life. He started walking back up the dirt road, back to the place where so long ago, it seemed, he had left his truck. As he neared the end of the dirt road, he could see the paved street of Beam Avenue and, beyond the trees, the front end of his truck. As he drew nearer to the paved road, his entire vehicle came into view. Sitting behind his truck was a car. A police car. Nathaniel made his way to the policeman seated in the squad car.

"This is my truck. What seems to be the problem, Officer?"

The policeman had his window rolled up and had not seen Nathaniel coming. Nathaniel's voice startled him, and he dropped the pen and clipboard that had been in his hands. Glaring at Nathaniel, he angrily got out of his car. He was middle-aged and short as policemen go, shorter than Nathaniel's five feet ten inches. His mustache was neat and trimmed, unlike his physique, which was sloppy and overweight.

"What do you think you're doing, coming up on me like that? Do you think that's funny?" he growled accusingly.

"No, not at all, Officer, I didn't mean to startle you," Nathaniel answered trying to hide a smile that wanted to spread across his face.

The officer narrowed his eyes and peered at Nathaniel suspiciously, looking him up and down. "What in the world have you been doing? How'd you get yourself looking like that?"

"Like what? What do you mean?" Nathaniel wondered before he caught his reflection in the police car's window. His hair was a mess, and leaves and bits of compost were stuck to his clothes. The start of a healthy black beard was upon his face. Nathaniel could do nothing but laugh at the sight of himself. He really didn't know what to say.

"I suppose you would not understand if I cried out, 'Repent, for I am the voice that cries from the wilderness!' would you?" Nathaniel asked lightheartedly. The policeman did not look amused.

"I'm sorry, Officer; let me explain. You see, my truck stalled here, for no apparent reason at all. Well, there really was a reason, I suppose, but that would make things too complicated. It was dark and I became disoriented. Well, I really wasn't disoriented; it was just that everything around me had changed," he excitedly told to the officer, who began to eye him warily. Nathaniel decided at this point that both of them would be better off if he cut his story short without too much detail. "Well, I ended up waking up here."

The policeman was unmoved by his story. He grimaced and shook his head back and forth. "You've been drinking or taken some kind of drug, haven't you? Imagine that, on Easter Sunday of all days. Let me see some I.D." Nathaniel took out his wallet and handed him his driver's license.

"Easter? Easter Sunday? How could that be?" Nathaniel asked, a look of astonishment on his face. "Are you sure it's Easter Sunday?"

"That's what I said," he stated impassively, letting out a grunt of discomfort as he bent down into his car, grabbing his clipboard and pen off the front seat. "Did you know it's illegal to park on this street overnight? I'm afraid I'm going to have to write you out a ticket," he barked, ending the sentence with a snort of indignation.

Nathaniel walked over to his truck and leaned up against the back of it. A delightful smile was on his face as he began picking and brushing the assorted debris off his body. "Can you imagine that; it's Easter Sunday, of all days. Well, what do you know about that!" Nathaniel felt almost giddy.

A few moments later, the policeman came back. "Here you are, Mr. O'Brien, happy Easter," the officer grumbled as he handed Nathaniel a ticket and his driver's license. "Your driving record show's no D.U.I.'s and I smell no alcohol on you. Your eyes appear clear, so maybe you're not on anything. Maybe you're just crazy," he remarked, chuckling at his own witticism.

"God bless you, Officer."

"Yeah, right. Well, hop in your truck. You said that it had stalled. Let's see if you can get it started."

Nathaniel hopped into his truck and turned the key. Without any hesitation at all, the engine came to life. The officer walked up to the driver's side window, shook his head and smirked, "I was right, you're just crazy."

"Thank you, sir; thank you for your help. I'll remember you in my prayers!" The policeman winced, and Nathaniel went happily on his way.

Nathaniel looked down at the ticket in his hand as he drove, "It says its 11:25 a.m. on the ticket. I know where I'm going to go. I know exactly where I'm going to go!" He turned on his directional signal and headed south.

Twenty minutes later, he pulled into the parking lot. Only a few cars were left, for Mount Calvary's Sunday morning services ended at 11:30 a.m. Nathaniel headed for the back of the lot and went through the back door, toward Charlie Fitch's office.

"Is that you honey? I'll be done in just a few minutes," Charlie Fitch shouted from his office as he heard Nathaniel walking toward his room.

"No, it's me, Nathaniel O'Brien."

Charlie Fitch's face went pale as he looked up uneasily from some pamphlets he was studying at his desk. "Wha… what do you want? Why are you here?" he asked meekly, his eyes searching Nathaniel's body for any kind of weapon.

"Charlie, I've come here today to apologize. I was wrong in the way I acted, and during the past few days I've discovered that you're not really my enemy. I'm sorry for the things I said, and if I hurt you in any way."

Charlie, after realizing Nathaniel was not there to harm him, regained his composure quickly. "Well, I should say so; I should say so," he huffed as he straightened himself and his expensive suit in his chair. "Were you aware of what you did to me, Mr. O'Brien?" he asked as he held up his left arm and pulled down his sleeve. His hand, wrist and arm were wrapped with an elastic bandage.

Nathaniel was startled. "I'm sorry… I had no idea I had hurt you so badly. I feel terrible about this. Send me any of the doctor bills that you've incurred or receive, and I'll be glad to pay them."

"Well, luckily for you there was no professional medical treatment needed. I've doctored this myself. I hope this makes you happy!" he huffed, grim-faced. Of course, it did not make Nathaniel happy. But in reality it did bring a sense of pleasure to Charlie Fitch, who really was feeling no pain in his arm. He enjoyed seeing the sense of shame on

Nathaniel's face, not to mention how the sight of his bandaged arm drew great sympathy from his congregation. Charlie was intent on milking that for all it was worth.

"You realize, Mr. O'Brien, that this is a serious matter, a matter I have solemnly weighed and considered, but have decided at this time not to press charges against you," he lectured, even raising one eyebrow to convey the graveness of the matter. This statement also had some basis in reality. Charlie indeed did not plan to press charges, but only after discovering from his attorney that he really had no case, since a small crowd of witnesses had seen him first attack Nathaniel, who had only reacted in self defense.

"Thank you Reverend Fitch, that's very kind of you. I want you to know that I see things differently now. It does no one any good for me to hate you or for you to hate me. What does that show a person who might be considering giving his life to Jesus? What does that do to the saints around us in church? We are imperfect; but if we have the spirit of God within us, how can we justify hating anyone? Its only God's spirit that can conquer our hate and division, our lusts and desires, our pride and envy. It is only God who can conquer and hold in check the forces that work tirelessly to confuse and bewilder us, for they take great delight in our bickering and fighting. They stir the fires that dwell within us all, hoping that if the fire becomes large enough it will consume not only that person but also the people around him. Our one and only hope, Reverend Fitch, is to pray. So that his will and his spirit will not only strengthen us, but cause our enemies to flee. I will pray for you Reverend Fitch, and for the church, that God's perfect will be done here."

Charlie Fitch sat speechless behind his desk. He didn't know whether it was Nathaniel's spirit or his words, but something seemed to reach him, past all his blustering and false bravado. He looked deep into Nathaniel's eyes and saw the love of Christ in them. Nathaniel stepped forward and extended his hand across the desk and shook Charlie's hand.

"I'll be going now, and I won't be back. But maybe we'll run into each other one of these days. Who knows, maybe some day we'll sit down together for a cup of coffee and a piece of pie." Nathaniel turned and walked out the door. Charlie Fitch sat there saying nothing, because for the first time in a long, long time, he could think of nothing to say.

Nathaniel stepped outside into the parking lot just as the sun came out from behind a cloud. He didn't know where he would go to church now, but he was sure he'd find one that suited him. He had learned that his walk with God was a personal one and did not depend on the frailties and failings of men. He walked to his truck and dug into his pants pocket for the keys. As he pulled them out, his eyes fell upon the skeleton key that Reverend McDermit had given him so long ago. He held it up and read out loud:

Greater is he that is in me, than he that is in the world.

"You know, Reverend, you were right all along. You tried to tell me then, but I just couldn't understand. But I do now." Nathaniel got into his truck and put the keys into the ignition. He paused and a big smile came across his face.

"Ethan, I don't know if you can hear me or not, but thanks. I'll be seeing you again some day, and if it's possible, tell Reverend McDermit I'm doing all right." With that, Nathaniel started his truck and drove away.

About the Author

Anthony Ducklow is an inner city school teacher whose teaching methods and work with his students have been featured in the *Saint Paul Pioneer Press* newspaper. He also created and appears in the award-winning television program, *Captain McCool and Friends*. He is a graduate of Northwestern College and Concordia College in St. Paul, Minnesota.

Where Angels Tread is a story that began taking shape after Mr. Ducklow heard a minister speculate on what might have transpired in the spiritual realm during the crucifixion of Jesus Christ. Years later, while attending Northwestern College, a professor's personal account of church conflict and the ensuing stories shared by fellow students provided him with ideas for the plot of the story. The novel is intended to give readers of all faiths not only a glimpse of the cross and the power that can be found there, but also of the danger of basing one's faith on fallible humans.